I0691917

MURDER BY ACCIDENT

a novel by

Barbara J. Olexer

Joyous Publishing
Milwaukie, Oregon, U.S.A.

Cover photo: Peter Skene Ogden State Scenic Viewpoint, courtesy Oregon Parks and Recreation Department

Copyright © 2009
by Barbara J. Olexer

All rights reserved. No part of this book may be reproduced in any form, except for the inclusion of brief quotations in a review, without permission in writing from the author.

Although the geographic places in this book are real places, all the characters are imaginary and any resemblance to any actual person, whether living or not, is purely accidental.

16-point Large Print

ISBN 978-0-9800514-5 -2

Joyous Publishing
9752 SE 43rd Avenue, Unit D
Milwaukie, Oregon 97222-1717
www.joyouspub.com

Printed in the U.S.A.

by Barbara J. Olexer

NONFICTION

Presidential Education: Prelude to Power
The Enslavement of the American Indian
in Colonial Times
Murder of a Soul: The Story of
Captain Jack (screenplay)
What Astrology Means to You: A Handbook of
Astrological Terms, Glyphs, and Applications

FICTION

They Lived Ever After
Death Takes a Flyer
Murder by Accident
If You Can't Trust Your Uncle Sam
Father to the Man
Fossil Rocks
Criminal Justice

Chapter 1

"Okay, Marge, take the rail," directed Paul Crittenden.

I cued the mare and she obediently moved to the outside of the riding arena, next to the fence that separated the arena from the grandstand on one long side. The mare walked smoothly and gracefully. She was a three-year-old leopard Appaloosa with a friendly disposition and plenty of spunk. Paul had named her Lotsa Spots but usually called her Spot.

"At the trot," Paul called.

This was my first real riding lesson and I hadn't ridden at all for several years so I felt a little insecure at the trot. Lotsa Spots sensed it and was reluctant to obey the cue.

"You'll have to be firm," Paul advised. "You've asked her to trot; keep at it until she does. You have to be the boss, you know.

I nodded and squeezed my legs into the mare's barrel. Lotsa Spots began to trot and Paul kept calling directions and advice from the center of the arena. Gradually, I gained confidence and relaxed somewhat. I could see it was going to be great fun to ride once I got to be really proficient. I'd ridden my cousins' horses when we were all kids and I had visited them in Camp Five, up in the foothills of the Blue Mountains of Oregon, but I had not been taught how to ride, beyond Uncle Miles telling me a few of the basics such as mounting from the left, or near, side and pulling back on the reins to slow or stop the horse. That kind of riding had been pleasant but I was beginning to suspect that it bore about the same relationship to disciplined riding as sandlot baseball to the major league game.

I had just taken my first teaching job after graduating from Southern Oregon College of Education. My parents had died in a boating accident during my senior year and my older brother and sister were married with families, so there was nothing to hold me in the old home town of Heppner. When Uncle Miles and Aunt Genevieve mentioned that a teacher was needed for the fifth, sixth, seventh, and eighth grades in the two-room school at Camp Five, I had decided to take on the challenge. There were ten scholars, or rather two scholars and eight pupils in the upper four grades. The Miller twins, Debbie and Dottie, were the only scholars in the school and it kept me busy finding projects to occupy their far-ranging inquisitiveness.

Camp Five was a logging camp that boasted a population of right around one hundred people. It was a sort of suburb to the lumber mill town of Kinzua, eleven miles away. Life at Camp Five was full and I had a satisfactory social life but I had begun to feel the need of a new interest. I had always loved the woods so with the entire scope of the Blue Mountains before me, I had decided to try horseback riding. My cousin Phil is a professional rodeo rider so I had asked him to recommend someone trustworthy to sell me a good horse at a manageable price and give me some lessons. Phil had sent me to Paul Crittenden of the Happy Appy Ranch a few miles out of Bend.

Paul was a lovely old man. In his nineties in the middle of the twentieth century, as a young man he had been into just about every endeavor available in the west. He'd worked on a fishing boat out of Coos Bay, been a lumberjack in the Siskiyous, been a fight promoter in the Sacramento Valley, and tended bar at the Bucket of Blood Saloon in Virginia City, Nevada. He had struck it rich during World War II. Lucky Lindy's flight over the Atlantic had made a deep impression on him and during the late thirties he'd turned his formidable energies to flying. He took some lessons but didn't really enjoy piloting. What he was interested in was the process of flying, all the little gizmos that made it possible to lift a plane off the ground and into the clouds. He was living in California at the time and when he invented some kind of gadget that solved a fairly important problem, he took it to the right person at the right time and got it patented and in production just in time for the war.

Having made a ton or so of money on his gadget and some other parts he manufactured, he sold out after the war and retired to a ranch in his native Oregon. By the time I met him, he was a widower and his three children had married and scattered across the country. He was tall and rangy, with all the marks of his active and eventful life. He was white-haired, what there was of it, and the skin of his face and hands and the little v-shaped spot left bare by his shirt were deeply tanned and weathered. The wrinkles in his face fell into laugh lines around his mouth and squint lines around his eyes from a refusal to wear sunglasses, which he considered sissyfied.

Paul and I had taken to one another at first sight. We'd talked a little while on the front porch of his ranch house, which was very nearly a mansion. It dated from the 1890s and had been built by a wealthy Easterner as a hunting lodge. The porch ran around three sides of the house, shading the windows in the summer. It was three stories tall with a mansard roof and a couple of porches built into the second story. Some of the windows were bordered with panels of stained glass. I wanted to make a tour of the house so bad I could taste it but couldn't think of any way to ask without seeming rude.

We went out to look over the stock and I was rather taken by a big white and brown gelding but Paul had firmly vetoed him and told me I really wanted Lotsa Spots. I wasn't totally convinced but I could see from the set of Paul's jaw that I might as well give Spot a try. So here I was in the big indoor arena, doing my best to make a good impression.

"Bring her down to a walk," Paul called.

I brought the mare back to a walk and then to a stop. Spot stopped carefully so as not to disturb my balance. Paul walked over and I dismounted.

"She's a lovely horse," I said, stroking the mare's withers.

Paul took the reins from me and patted the mare's neck. "Yes, she's a right nice little filly. Just the ticket for you. Plenty of spirit and no vice a-tall."

"I'd need some lessons, you know," I told him.

He snorted. "I can see that. Tell you what, you come back tomorrow morning and I'll give you a lesson and then we can talk more to the point. Because if you haven't got it in you to be a fine rider, you're not going to get a Happy Appy horse."

I smiled at him. "Okay. That seems reasonable. What time tomorrow morning do you want me?"

"Six. That'll give us time for a lesson and some get-acquainted time and time to make the deal, if it works out that way."

I groaned inwardly. I'd have to be up by five in order to get to the ranch by six. On a Sunday morning, too. Well, if that's what it took, I'd just have to make the best of it.

"All right."

Paul led the mare out of the arena, back to her stall. I watched as he took off the saddle and bridle and checked to make sure water was available and that her headstall and lead shank were hanging by the stall door. He threw the bridle over his shoulder and picked up the saddle. His movements were sure and deft, although age had slowed him. Depositing the tack in its room, he closed the door and started for the house.

It was dark outside but the yard light illuminated the area. As we came out of the barn, a young man came down the walk from the house and we stopped to talk with him.

"Marge, this is my grandson, Laine. Marge

O'Connor. She's interested in buying a horse and learning to ride."

Laine gave me a friendly smile and wanted to shake hands, so we did. He was built like his grandfather but his facial features were cast in a much different mold. He was round-faced with hazel eyes; pleasant looking but not handsome.

"You've come to the right place, Miss O'Connor. Grandpa's the best teacher in the whole Northwest."

"That's what my cousin said. I think you know him. Phil O'Connor?"

"Sure. Sure, Phil and I used to rodeo together until I got too old. I haven't seen him in a coon's age. How is the old boy?"

"He's more or less okay. Seems as if he's always healing up after breaking something. He's still rodeoing, you know."

"No kidding. I'd like to see old Phil, he ever come around these parts?"

"Not too often. He'll be at Pendleton, of course."

"I haven't been for a couple of years. Maybe I'll go this year and look him up. Talk about old times."

Paul snorted. "Old times. Listen to you. Ain't but a yearling and talking about old times. You want to hear about old times, I'll tell you someday when I ain't got anything better to do."

"I wish you would," Laine said. "You haven't told

7

me half the good stories I know you've got stored away." He turned to me. "He says he doesn't want to turn into an old bore so he doesn't talk about his younger days much."

"Maybe we can persuade him," I said. "I'd love to hear your stories, Mr. Crittenden. Fifty or sixty years ago sounds like a much more romantic time than now."

"Romantic." Paul thought about it. "Maybe. Maybe it sounds romantic. But that's just because it's long enough ago that the misery's gone out of it. Only the love and excitement and beauty are left."

"I expect you're right. But I do want to hear your stories." I went over to my Pontiac.

"See you in the morning, Marge," Paul said as I got behind the wheel.

"You bet," I said. "Six a.m. sharp."

"Six?" Laine grinned at me. "Couldn't you talk him into a more civilized hour?"

"I didn't try. One look at that jaw and I knew I was no match for him."

Laine and Paul laughed.

"Smart woman, huh, Grandpa? It took the rest of us years to come to that conclusion."

Paul shot him a look. "Even now some of you have to be reminded." He turned back to me. "All right, missy, I'll see you in the morning."

8

"I'll be here." I started the car, smiled at both men and drove away.

Finding myself in town with nothing to do for the afternoon and evening, I decided to go shopping. There wasn't anything I absolutely needed but it was nice to get out and see what there was to see. Camp Five, of course, had only a tiny branch of the company store. Kinzua, eleven miles away, had the main company store and it sold everything from groceries to dry goods but there wasn't much selection. Otherwise, the nearest shopping was forty miles away in Heppner one direction and twenty or thirty miles away in Fossil and Condon the other. Even then the shopping didn't amount to much.

I showered and changed out of jeans and cotton shirt into a woolen skirt and cashmere sweater. Then I drove downtown and indulged in a couple of hours of mostly window shopping. I did buy a couple of western shirts -- mother-of-pearl buttons, pointed yokes, and all. There was a tack shop filled with all sorts of leather goods -- saddles, bridles, hobbles, and chaps of all kinds. I was very tempted by some silver concho belts and silver and turquoise jewelry for both people and horses but I restrained myself and escaped without buying anything. I was on the way back to the car when I fell victim to a window display in a fabric shop. Bolts of rich, shimmery,

9

jewel-colored satin brocade and bolts of deep, dusky tones of voluptuous velvet cascaded across a show window. I stood and gazed, mesmerized by the beauty of the fabrics. I have always had a weakness for lovely fabrics. I imagined myself trailing down wide stone stairs gowned in flowing velvet overlaying satin brocade with wide ruffles of soft lace at throat and wrists. Then I laughed. Yes, imagine trailing across the dance floor at the Odd Fellows Hall in a get-up of velvet and satin and lace. Some picture.

I went inside the store. The velvets had a fine hand, supple and soft but with body. The brocades also had a nice hand, thick and smooth. I knew I had no business to buy fabrics like these. There are few, if any, occasions in my life that could possibly call for gowns of satin brocade. I might use velvet for winter weddings, holiday parties, that sort of thing. Or maybe a suit of brocade with a lace blouse. In the end I walked out of the store with several yards of velvets and brocades that I had absolutely no common sense reason for buying.

The Deschutes River runs through Bend, tumbling swiftly and spectacularly over boulders, foaming and splashing and sparkling. I had been lucky enough to get a room at the motel down by the river, actually overlooking a stretch of rapids. The river was high with the spring runoff so it was not as wild-looking as it would be later in the summer. Still, it was swirling dizzily and I sat at the window for a while, watching the floodlit untamed water force its way north through the mountains to join the Columbia. The growling of my stomach brought me back to mundane considerations and I realized that I was hungry and decided to treat myself to dinner and a movie. After all, here I was in the city on a Friday night; I might as well enjoy the bright lights.

There was a Chinese restaurant where I used to stop on my way home from college -- they made an incredibly delicious egg foo yung. I have never traveled out of the country, certainly never to the Orient, but I knew that the egg foo yung served at that restaurant in Bend was Americanized to the nth degree and was probably unrecognizable to the Chinese. Still, I always felt that I was in an exotic foreign milieu when I sat in one of those red booths, drinking tea from a tiny handle-less cup, looking at the elaborate pictures made of mother-of-pearl and embroidery. It was all so very different from Camp Five.

The movie was a Robert Mitchum film noir. There again, it was exotic and foreign. I had visited several big cities outside of Oregon -- San Francisco, Los Angeles, San Diego, Chicago, Denver, and even

Washington, D.C. Our high school teacher for history and social studies, Mr. Devane, had organized a bus trip back east when I was a junior. We were gone almost three weeks and did we have a time! But in none of the cities I had ever visited, had I seen anything like the life portrayed in the movie. It seemed perfectly reasonable while Robert Mitchum went about his duties as a homicide detective but outside the theater, walking back to the car, it seemed as unreal as the man in the moon.

I was up at five the next morning, and by five-forty I was in jeans and one of the new western shirts with a Pendleton shirt as a jacket, and on my way out to the Happy Appy Ranch. I didn't bother about breakfast, not being accustomed to eating in the middle of the night. I parked and went directly to the barn. I was a few minutes early but Paul was already there, brushing Lotsa Spots preparatory to tacking her up.

"Good morning," I sang out.

Paul turned and smiled. "Good morning yourself, missy. Right cheery this morning, aren't you?"

"I am that. It's a beautiful day. I have a date with my best guy and he's going to teach me all the subtle nuances of western equitation."

Paul snorted. "Equitation. I can teach you to ride but you'll have to equitate on your own. Bring me that saddle we had on her yesterday."

"Right." I turned toward the tack room.

"And the bridle, too. It's hanging right over the saddle."

"Okay." I went into the tack room, hoping I could recognize the saddle. I very much wanted Paul's liking and respect. Luckily, the saddle was easy to spot; it was the only one with a suede seat. I threw the bridle and reins over my shoulder and picked up the saddle and saddle blanket, kicking the door closed behind me.

Paul took the saddle blanket and placed it on Spot then set the saddle in place. "Here, you cinch her up. Stooping ain't as easy for age as it is for beauty."

I reached under Spot's belly for the girth and pulled it through the ring, snugly but not tightly. When I finished, I stepped back and looked at Paul for his verdict. He slipped two fingers between the girth and the horse and nodded.

"Not too bad. Let's see you put the bridle on her."

Now, I have never liked bridling a horse. I always seem to annoy the animal so it gets to tossing its head around. This time, to my great relief, Spot accepted the bridle and allowed me to slip the bit into her mouth.

Paul watched critically. "All right. But here, let me show you something." He held his hand up over

Spot's poll with his thumb and little finger spread as if holding a headstall. "Hold it up like this and position it. Then lower it so the bit is right in front of her mouth. Put your other thumb in her mouth like this and when she opens, slip the bit in and pull the headstall up and settle it over her ears. Nice and smooth. I see you know better than to bang her teeth with the bit. That'll irritate any horse and make 'em hard to tack up."

"I'll remember."

"Okay, lead her into the arena."

Paul put both of us through our paces for an hour. At the end of it, I had begun to appreciate Lotsa Spots and was anxious to continue the lesson. But Paul said we both needed a break.

"No sense in pushing till you get stale the first day," Paul said. "Come on in the house and have some breakfast."

"If it wouldn't be any trouble, I would like a cup of coffee."

"Won't be any trouble for me," the old man chuckled. "I'm not going to make it or serve it. Come on and meet Ricki, my housekeeper. If you're going to hang around here, you'd better get on her good side. Folks think I'm the boss but she's the cook and let me tell you, it's always the cook who's the real boss."

I laughed. "I expect you're right about that."

Paul watched while I put Spot in her stall and put the tack away. Luckily, I remembered to check the water bucket. The mare had not worked so hard that a lengthy cool down was necessary.

Following Paul's example, I carefully scraped my boots and wiped them on the mat before going up the steps to the back door. As soon as Paul opened the kitchen door, the aroma of baking biscuits and frying bacon streamed out and engulfed us. Suddenly I was ravenously hungry.

"Hey, Ricki-Tikki, I've brought another victim to eat your cooking," Paul announced. "This is Marge O'Connor. Marge, this is housekeeper, chief cook and bottle-washer, and the kingpin of this establishment, Mrs. Ricki Fenton."

Ricki smiled and turned toward us while she continued turning slices of bacon in a large frying pan.

"Come ahead in," she invited. "I'm just about to take some biscuits out of the oven. Just put your jacket on a chair. The lavatory is through there, if you'd like to wash your hands."

"Thanks." As I hung my Pendleton shirt on the back of one of the kitchen chairs, I noticed that the table was set for four, and went through the indicated door.

When I came back, Paul motioned for me to sit down. "Sit in, sit in," he said. "I'll be right with you."

He disappeared through the door and I stood uncertainly, watching Ricki bustle about. The rich aroma of fresh coffee joined the other delightful smells and set my mouth salivating. Ricki was the busiest woman I had ever seen. Short and plump, with a ruddy complexion and dark hair permed into poodle curls, she was perpetually in motion. She went from sink to stove to counter to table to refrigerator to cupboard in a seemingly endless quest for everything one could conceivably want or need for a simple breakfast.

"Sit down, Miss O'Connor," Ricki said, as she swished past with a jar of homemade jam. "I hope you like peach preserves. If not, I have apple butter and raspberry jelly and elderberry jam and..."

I interrupted. "I do like peach preserves. But, please, don't go to any extra trouble on my account."

Ricki pried the paraffin seal off and spooned the preserves into a cut glass dish. She set the dish on the table and took the butter dish out of the cupboard and put that on the table. Paul came in and sat at the head of the table.

"Good gosh, woman," he said, winking at me, "haven't you got breakfast ready yet?"

"You just hold your horses, Paul. It's almost

16

ready."

Although I was sure I already knew the answer, I asked, "Is there anything I can do to help?"

Ricki stopped for an instant and gave me a look of astonishment. "Why, no. I think I've got everything under control, Miss O'Connor."

That was just about what I expected but courtesy demanded that I make the offer. "Please, call me Marge," I said.

Ricki flew across the room to the refrigerator and said over her shoulder, "All right." She took a small carton from the refrigerator and poured cream into a silver cream pitcher. Then she flitted to the stove for potholders and extracted the biscuits. She went over to the dish cupboard for a plate and back to the stove to pile biscuits onto it. She delivered the plate to the table and went back to the counter and began to break eggs into a bowl.

I was getting slightly dazed with all the whirlwind of activity. Paul was amused.

"Wears you out just watching her, doesn't it?"

I looked at him doubtfully, wondering if I should answer. I was glad when Ricki created a diversion and I didn't have to.

She turned, briskly beating the eggs with a fork. "Marge, would you just step across the hall and tell Laine that breakfast is ready?" She nodded her head

17

toward the hall, then turned and poured the eggs into a pan on the stove.

"Oh, sure," I said and jumped up. "Glad to."

Out in the hall there were several choices. The door to the lavatory was directly across from the kitchen door. The door next to the kitchen opened into the dining room. The stairs rose in a sweeping curve and beyond them the hall widened into a foyer. The front door had a big oval of glass etched with a magnificent stag with an impossibly luxuriant rack of antlers and long stained glass panels on either side of it. Between the front door and the stairs, on either side of the foyer, were double doors, the kind that slide back into the wall, to make a double parlor when they are all open. I tried the set on the left first, tapping lightly before sliding one of the doors back. That turned out to be the living room, comfortably furnished and gleaming with high gloss polishes of various kinds. A tap on the door to the right was answered by a friendly roar.

"Come in."

I opened the door to find myself in an office. Laine sat at a rolltop desk working in a bookkeeping ledger. Columns of figures marched across the pages. He looked up and grinned.

"Well, yes, indeed. Come right in, Miss O'Connor."

"Mrs. Fenton sent me to tell you that breakfast is ready. And please, call me Marge."

"All right." He dropped his pencil on the ledger. "Come on, I'm starving."

He jumped up and hurried me down the hall and back to the kitchen.

As we ate, I could feel the friendliness begin to turn into friendship. These were my kind of people and I began to feel at home in their midst. It was getting on for nine o'clock when the meal finally ended. Ricki firmly refused any help with clearing up.

"Laine," Paul suggested, "why don't you take Marge for a drive? Show her around some?"

Chapter 2

Laine and I climbed into his pickup and drove out to the highway. He stopped at the cattle guard.

"Which way? Anything particular you'd like to see?"

"Well, I've lived in eastern Oregon all my life, except for college in Ashland, but I've never spent much time right here around Bend. Why don't you show me the places you love best? Only, I'm already pretty well acquainted with sagebrush."

Laine laughed. "Yeah, me, too." He turned right onto the blacktop. "It's a little too muddy to get out on the dirt roads, which is where I really want to go, but we can take the gravel roads."

We drove through the ranch, Laine pointing out things like the place he and his friends had a tree house when he was a kid and the place in the creek where he and his cousins had learned to swim. I thought the Happy Appy must be one of the most beautiful and blessed places on earth. It seemed to have everything, a pristine creek splashing through meadows and woods, little copses of quaking aspens dotted here and there along the creek, vistas of long slopes of evergreens stretching up to snowline.

I got my directions kind of turned around so I was surprised when we struck Highway 97 north of Bend. We crossed Crooked River and I shivered as I looked down the gorge from the bridge -- the river was eight hundred feet below. I told Laine how my dad used to stop and drop wooden kitchen matches over the cliff so we could marvel that when they struck the rocks, they lighted. He laughed and said his grandfather used to do the same when he was young.

We compared tall stories we'd been told as children; how the side-hill gougers wore narrow switchback trails on the hillsides because their legs on one side were longer than on the other; how when the story teller was young, he didn't bother to shave, just bit the whiskers off on the inside. And the Paul Bunyan tales. How one winter it got so cold that when the guys talked in the bunkhouse, the words froze before they could get to the other guys' ears so they just tossed the frozen words behind the stove and what a racket it made come spring and they all thawed out. We laughed and I began to feel as if I'd known Laine forever.

Then we talked about our histories and I told him about my mom and dad being killed in a boating accident my senior year in college. I told him about my brother and sister and their families. And he told me something of his family.

Laine was the only offspring of Paul's middle child, his son Mace, and Mace's first wife, Georgia. His parents had been divorced when he was very young so while he was growing up, he'd spent the school year with his mother in various towns all around the west and his summers with Paul. I felt sorry for him but didn't think it would be wise to tell him so. Laine himself didn't seem to think there was anything sad about his childhood. His father owned a pear orchard and a fruit packing plant near Medford in the Rogue River Valley. He had re-married seven or eight years ago, and had a six-year-old son and a four-year-old daughter by his second wife, Agnes. Agnes had two daughters, now in their teens. By his tone of voice, Laine didn't care much for his father's second family, which wasn't at all surprising.

Laine's mother had just moved back to this area. She bought a little resort up in the mountains on the Deschutes. More of a motel, really, Laine amended, than a resort, just the right size for her to run and although it felt really remote it was only about an hour from Bend.

He told me a little about his aunts, Paul's other two children. The older aunt, Elmyra Boggs, had a son and a daughter, both grown now. The younger aunt, Lorena Winton, had two daughters, also grown up. Elmyra lived in Reno and Lorena lived back east, somewhere in Kansas. None of them spent much time at the ranch and Laine didn't sound as if he missed them.

I ventured to ask how he came to be living there.

"Oh, I just kind of drifted into it. I always thought of the ranch as home and when Grandpa began to get old the last three or four years, I started spending more and more time with him. Finally, he offered me a partnership if I'd come permanently. I didn't have a career or anything so I took him up on it. Actually, I love the life."

"I can see that. I can see you love your grandfather, too."

Laine shot me a glance of surprise. "Well, sure. He's a great old guy."

He stopped at a fork in the road. "My mother's place is not too far from here. Do you mind if we stop by for a few minutes?"

I didn't, of course, I'd been wondering how to get to meet Laine's mom. I was intrigued by his description of her and curious about the kind of woman who preferred independence to marriage. In a few minutes, Laine took a right turn off the highway onto a narrow black-topped road that climbed gently but steadily up into the mountains. The woods grew thicker and taller and more beautiful the higher we went. After a few miles, the road dipped and dropped down to the Deschutes River.

The motel was situated in one of the loveliest spots on earth. We crossed the river on a log bridge and pulled off the road at a little log house that did duty as a motel office, grocery store, tackle shop, and home. An old-fashioned gas pump stood in front, the kind with a glass cylinder on top. There were a dozen or more log cabins scattered on the hillside among the trees, which were mostly tall old Douglas firs.

Laine parked beside the little store and when we opened the pickup doors we could hear the river crashing and splashing over the rocks. There was a rapids just past the bridge, on the upriver side, and the sun struck millions of tiny rainbows in the frothing water. I was just about to remark that here was a place truly deserving of being described as heaven on earth when the door flew open on Cabin Nine and a woman shot out, screaming like a fishwife.

The cause of her wrath was not immediately apparent. She came down the two steps to the path, turned, and began to wave her arms, punctuating her tirade. I was sorry for whoever was on the receiving end but at the same time it struck me as comical. She was a short, fat woman dressed in a faded blue print housedress and white crepe-soled shoes. I couldn't see the color of her hair because she had tied a red and yellow flowered scarf around her head so that all her hair was covered.

As she stood on the path screaming vituperation, a very young couple emerged from the cabin, the girl carrying an overnight case and her purse, the boy carrying a suitcase. They tried to break into the torrent of abuse coming from the woman but to no avail. Stony-faced, they stowed their bags in the trunk of a late model Lincoln convertible and drove off, leaving two little bald patches where their tires had spun and dug up the mat of conifer needles. The woman scowled after the car for a moment then turned her attention to us, retaining the scowl until she recognized her son.

"Laine," she exclaimed with a radiant smile. "I wasn't expecting you today."

Laine grinned at her and gave her a kiss on the cheek.

"I don't see why not, I come over most Saturdays. Mom, I'd like you to meet Marge O'Connor. Miss O'Connor, this is my mother, Georgia Crittenden."

I smiled at her and told her I was glad to meet her; she echoed my words but without any pleasure that I could see.

"Come on in," she said. "I've got time for a little visit before I have to get back to work. Penny let me down today so I've got to tend to everything."

As she talked she led the way into the store building by the back door. We went through the kitchen into a small living room and she waved us to chairs.

"Just let me take my 'back in 10 minutes' clock off the front door."

She went on through an open door into the store and we heard the little bell that was attached to the top of the door frame as the door opened and closed. The room was positively claustrophobic. It was crammed with a jumble of antique furniture, oil lamps, china, framed fashion pages from *Godey's Ladies Book*, old pharmaceutical implements, and a miscellany of ornaments. There was a glass case jammed full of salt and pepper shakers made in the likeness of everything from Generals Lee and Grant (Lee was salt, Grant was pepper) to the Democratic donkey and the Republican elephant (the donkey was salt, the elephant was pepper).

"I haven't had a minute to think this morning," Mrs. Crittenden said, sitting down in a bentwood

26

rocking chair. "First it was Penny sending word that she was sick and wouldn't be able to come to work. Penny Ludlow," she explained to me, her breathing quick and heavy, "is the chambermaid. When she bothers to show up, that is."

"I thought she was doing all right," Laine said. "Last Saturday you seemed to be pleased with her."

"Last Saturday she came to work," his mother snapped. "I've had all the cabins to clean and beds to make this morning, besides opening the store at 5:00 A.M. for the fishermen. This is the first time I've been able to sit down and catch my breath since before five."

"Didn't you take time to eat breakfast? You know you ought to start the day out right, especially busy days."

"Well, of course I had breakfast," Mrs. Crittenden declared. "I can't do everything around here without sustenance. But this morning, that was just one more chore, cooking breakfast and then having to do up the dishes. Then, as if I didn't have enough on my hands, those people in Nine who were leaving when you drove up were late checking out. The signs on the doors in all the cabins state perfectly plainly that check out time is noon and they'll be charged for another day if they don't get out in time. So I went over there and told them they'd have to pay for another day but all I got for my trouble was smart aleck remarks. Plus, I don't even think they are married. The girl had a ring on her finger but it looked to me like an ordinary ring turned so the setting was inside her hand. If I'd seen it last night when they checked in, they wouldn't have got a room and I told them so. But she didn't come in last night, just him. He wouldn't pay for today, either, just said he didn't see that a half hour over the limit entitled me to a whole night's rent. It doesn't matter if it's a half hour or the whole day, the sign says twelve noon is check out time and that's what it means. These rich city people come out here and think they're in the back of beyond and can do anything they please."

She paused for breath and Laine took the opportunity to offer to help her with the work and I offered to pitch in, as well. I had thought at first that her heavy breathing was the result of excitement and exercise but it changed very little after she sat down. I thought that just breathing that hard all day would wear her out; it made me tired just to hear her.

"Thank you, I appreciate your offer but Penny's older sister brought the message and she stayed and helped. You remember Sandy, don't you, Laine? You met her here one time when she came to pick Penny up. She'll be about finished with the other cabins and then she can do Nine."

My head was fairly swimming by the time she had offered us lunch and Laine had fibbed and said we'd already eaten and had to get back. She said there was something wrong with her car, it was getting hard to start, and Laine went to look at it. I asked to use her lavatory while he was gone and was graciously accorded permission, although cautioned not to waste water when I washed my hands.

When I went back into the living room, she was standing at the door to the store. I followed her through to the front door and we went out and stood in the sun. Laine joined us there in a few minutes. He told his mother that she needed a new battery and she wailed about the expense and not being able to afford it until he told her to go to the garage the ranch patronized in Bend and charge it to him, he'd tell them to expect her. She was all smiles after that until we climbed into the pickup cab and, smiling and waving, drove away.

"She's not really so bad," Laine said sheepishly. "She's had a hard time raising me by herself and having to work, too. It's made her kind of cranky but she's really good-hearted. She's always wanted to marry again but she's been too particular and hard to suit. I wish she would find someone she could marry so she could relax and not have to work so hard and have so much responsibility."

I agreed that it sounded as if she had had a hard time and held my tongue as to what I thought of her behavior. We stopped on the outskirts of Bend and had lunch before we headed back to the Happy Appy Ranch for my afternoon lesson. Laine took a roundabout way so he could show me some petroglyphs at the mouth of a partially collapsed lava tube. It was beginning to cloud over but he parked the pickup so the headlights illuminated the ancient figures.

We got out of the cab and walked over to the cave. Shallowly incised were outlines of mountain sheep and a few handprints but mainly there was a profusion of circles and dots, apparently incised at random over the surface of the cave wall.

I studied the carvings for a few minutes. I had seen petroglyphs in a couple of other places but I was always interested in them. No one could interpret them. No one knew who carved them or when or why. Present day Indians said they didn't know anything about them except that they had always been there.

"You know," I said, "it would have taken quite a while to carve these. I wonder who thought it was worth all the trouble. I wish I knew what they mean."

"No one seems to know," Laine said. "The Indians who were here when the whites first got here couldn't decipher them. They didn't know who carved them, either. They're all over the west, you know."

I nodded. A thought struck me. "But not back east?"

"I don't really know. I've never thought much about it."

"Well, I'm glad you showed them to me. I just wish I knew what they mean."

"Yeah, like you said, it would be too much work not to mean something." He turned back toward the pickup. "We'd better get back. Grandpa will be champing at the bit to give you your lesson. It doesn't do to keep him waiting."

I grinned. "I'm sure it doesn't."

We climbed back into the cab of the pickup and Laine backed around and onto the road once more.

"I'm going to take a little short cut home."

"Oh, no, not one of the infamous shortcuts," I exclaimed, in mock dismay.

Laine laughed. "I see you've taken shortcuts before."

"Not taken, been taken. I don't think I've ever been inveigled into taking one that turned out to save either time or distance."

"This one will save both. I've used it many times and I know it like the back of my hand."

I groaned. "Worse and worse. That's a perfect

description of disaster in the making. 'I know it like the back of my hand.' The last time I heard those words, we hadn't gone half a mile before the leader of the expedition had to confess himself completely lost."

"Well, obviously, he wasn't completely lost. I mean, here you are."

"He was completely lost -- it was my cousin Phil two or three years ago. We were camping on Steens Mountain and we'd ridden horseback from our camp at the top down to the Donner and Blitzen River. Then Phil said he knew a shortcut back."

"How on earth could you get lost there? All you had to do was ride uphill again."

"Yes, that's what I thought. But Phil said there was a more direct way. Naturally, my cousin Lorraine and I and a couple of others who were with us, let him lead. Until we realized we were completely around on the wrong side of the mountain with a sheer cliff in front of us. Then we deposed Phil and retraced our way back to the river and followed it upstream and then went on up to the top where we were camped. You've been to Steens Mountain?"

"Not yet. I hear it's something special and I'm going sometime."

"It is beautiful," I said, remembering the

gorgeous light and the way it played over the mountain. "It was the fall of the year when we were there and the aspens had turned color. I don't know of anything quite as lovely as a grove of aspens in the fall. The leaves seem to give off light instead of just reflecting it."

"They do, don't they? I don't know of any other tree that has the same kind of glow as the aspens."

A little silence fell but neither of us felt constrained to keep talking. The ride was a little rough over the graveled road but I was enjoying it. Suddenly, Laine slammed on the brakes and I had to catch myself against the dashboard. Looking around, I saw the reason he'd stopped.

"Oh, the poor little things," I cried.

A white-face cow was lying still at the foot of a thick old juniper tree. Two little calves were standing near her, looking lost and forlorn.

"We'll have to take them in," Laine said, opening his door and stepping out.

I grinned to myself as I stepped out of the cab. "How?"

"We'll catch them and put them in the pickup bed. They can't stay out here, they'll starve. If the coyotes don't get them first."

"Okay. Do you have a rope?"

"There should be one behind the seat."

There should have been but there wasn't.

"How are we going to catch them, then?" I asked.

"Run 'em down, I reckon."

And that's what we did. It took quite a little while with lots of slipping and sliding and a couple of falls in the mud for each of us. The calves didn't know what to do without their mother but they knew what they didn't want to do and that was to have anything to do with the two human berserkers who had happened by. Bawling and kicking, they darted here and there, twisting and turning to elude capture. We finally wore the calves down enough through hunger and exhaustion to catch them. Laine hoisted them up into the bed of the pickup and they promptly tried to climb out over the side.

"We could put them in the cab," I yelled over their bawling.

"Oh, no, not in my cab," Laine retorted grimly.

"Okay, I'll ride back here with them and keep them in."

Laine shot me a look of dark disapproval. "I'll do it. Can you drive the pickup?"

"I can. I'd rather you drove and I'll ride back here."

"No can do, lady. You drive."

Laine climbed over the side wearily and shooed the calves away from the sides of the pickup bed.

"Come on," he said, "let's go and get this over with."

I climbed into the cab and turned the ignition key. I was a little rusty, it having been a while since I'd driven a pickup but pretty soon the knack came back. Laine didn't have too bad a time in the back. When the pickup began to move, the terrified calves stopped trying to climb out and stood unsteadily in the center of the bed and bawled. At each place that the road offered a choice of directions, I looked back and Laine pointed out the right way.

Paul was on the front porch with a group of people when we drove into the yard. He hurried around the house to the back. A pastel pink Olds was parked beside Ricki's elderly blue Chevy.

"What the dickens are you doing?" Paul called, coming up to us as I parked near the corral, which was fortunately empty. "Have you taken to cattle rustling?"

I laughed and Laine grinned, as we got out of the pickup. The calves renewed their bawling.

"Nope. I'll tell you about it in a minute," Laine said, shooing the calves away from the side of the pickup bed where they were trying to climb out. "Marge, open the gate."

I opened the corral gate and hurried back to the pickup to help.

"You keep one of them in the pickup," Laine directed, "while I put the other one in the corral."

Paul went to the corral gate and when Laine had carried one of the calves over and deposited it inside, he closed the gate, opening it just enough to let Laine out again. I picked up the second calf and carried it over to the gate. Paul opened it and I put the calf in a little distance from the gate and scooted out when Paul opened it. We stood and watched the calves while Laine and I took turns explaining to Paul how we came to be playing nursemaid.

"I don't know what happened to their mother," Laine said. "She was just lying there dead. I couldn't see that she was wounded in any way."

"There weren't any signs of any kind of a scuffle," I added, puzzled anew as to what killed the cow.

"She probably ran into the juniper and broke her neck," Paul said.

"Maybe," Laine said skeptically.

"Cows *are* pretty dumb," I said, remembering various encounters I'd had with them. "And they panic easily. I saw one run slap into the side of a pickup one time. I thought at first she was charging us but I think really she was just so frightened that she was running blindly."

Paul nodded. "That's about the size of it, I reckon.

Cows are dumb and skittish. It's a poor combination. Laine, you want to call old George Nitchelm? They're most likely his calves and we sure aren't equipped to deal with a couple of bummer calves."

"Yeah, I'll do it right now. Little guys are starving. Who's that on the porch? I don't seem to recognize the car."

"Elmyra and Leroy. Brad come, too, and his girlfriend."

"How long are they staying?"

"I don't know. I didn't ask."

"Ricki'll be delighted," Laine said with a grimace.

He went to the house and Paul turned to me.

"Well, little lady, it's getting late. Let's get started on your lesson."

"Great," I said, smiling at him.

I tacked up the mare under Paul's watchful eye and led her into the arena.

He put us through a pretty tough workout for about an hour that afternoon. From the walk to the gallop, side-passing, figure eights, backing, and even a couple of low jumps. I noticed the arrival of a couple of people who stood and watched for awhile but I was too busy with the lesson to pay any attention to them.

Paul showed me how to hold the reins to cue Spot

by tightening and loosening my fingers instead of hauling back on them. He also told me that I need to stretch my Achilles tendons by exercising on a thick book so I could get my heels down where they belong. That sounded kind of weird and I wondered if he was teasing me. Something like the side-hill gouger or the great popcorn blizzard.

"I've got to go out and check on the windmill over at Rabbit Flat. You practice your side-passing and backing but don't do any jumping until I get back. I won't be gone long."

I nodded. I began to practice at once, cuing Spot to back, concentrating on holding the reins exactly right and using my legs the way Paul had told me. I heard a man's voice but didn't take particular notice of what he said.

"Grandpa, it's getting dark, can't it wait until tomorrow?"

"No, Brad, it can't. Stock has got to have water whether it's convenient or not. I check that windmill every afternoon and I'm going to check it this afternoon. You can come along, if you want."

"No, thanks. Marsha and I'll go on back to the house, see if anything's doing there."

"Suit yourself."

I saw Paul go out of the arena and a couple of minutes later I heard his pickup start. Then I took

Spot around the arena to the pole on the ground and positioned her to side-pass the length of it. I was so engrossed in practicing what Paul had taught me that I lost all track of time.

Chapter 3

Just as I finished putting Lotsa Spots in her stall and the saddle and bridle in the tack room, Laine came into the barn. The big double doors were closed so he came through the small, man-sized door cut into one of the big ones.

"Marge," he said, as soon as he was close enough to talk without shouting, "Brad said Grandpa went to check the windmill out at Rabbit Flat."

I was surprised. Laine seemed excited, apprehensive, but as far as I could see there was nothing to be either excited or apprehensive about.

"Yes, that's what he said to someone he called Brad."

"Brad was in here?"

I nodded. "He was watching Paul give me a lesson. There was someone with him, I think. I didn't pay much attention, I was concentrating on the lesson. But Paul told me to practice side-passing and backing but not to jump until he got back. That was quite a while ago and I'm about beat so I decided I'd leave word with you or Mrs. Fenton and go on back to the motel."

"How long ago did he leave?"

"I don't know. I didn't look at my watch."

"An hour, two hours?"

"I'm sorry, Laine. I just don't know."

"Okay. I'm going to go look for him. Rabbit Flat is only about a twenty-minute drive, even with the roads like this. He should have been back by now. If the windmill was jammed or anything, and he tried to fix it..."

Laine turned and started for the door. I hurried to catch up with him.

"What are you afraid of, Laine? That he's had a stroke or a heart attack or something?"

Laine nodded. "He had a minor heart attack a couple of years ago and the doctor warned him not to do anything strenuous. But you know Grandpa."

"May I go with you? If he's not okay, you may need some help with him. Oh." I caught myself and stopped, embarrassed. "I'm sorry, I don't mean to butt in. I guess with family here, some of them will want to go with you."

Laine snorted. He sounded just like Paul at that moment.

"I'd rather have you, if you don't mind going."

41

It was completely dark outside, except for the yard light. Laine held the door open and I climbed into the cab of his pickup. My purse was there on the seat; I'd forgotten all about it. Good thing I'd decided to come with Laine. Otherwise, I would have been without money, driver's license, car keys and the motel room key.

Laine took the gravel road too fast for comfort but his urgency had communicated itself to me. I held onto the seat with one hand and the elbow rest with the other and tried to see beyond the range of the headlights. The pickup slewed around curves and I caught glimpses of juniper trees spaced among the sagebrush. We rattled over a cattle guard and Laine shifted down as we immediately began to climb a grade.

"Listen." I had caught a faint sound that ought not to have been there. I rolled the window down and the cold night air billowed into the cab along with the alien sound, now a little louder. "Isn't that a car horn?"

"Yeah."

The sound got steadily louder and finally we could pinpoint the direction it was coming from, just ahead and to the left, down the slope. Laine pulled over as much as he could on the narrow road and parked. There was barely room for another vehicle to get by. He turned off the engine and the lights. He took a flashlight from the jockey box and we both jumped out. The wheels on my side were right at the edge of the road and I nearly fell as I dropped down below road level.

Laine flicked the flashlight on. The sagebrush loomed up huge in the light and then seemed to shrink back to normal size as the light passed over it. The slope was steep and the darkness made it seem steeper than it was.

"You'd better stay here, Marge," Laine said.

"No, I'm coming with you. There's obviously been an accident of some kind."

He took my hand and I let him lead me down the slope toward the sound of the horn. That was one of the most dismal sounds I have ever heard. We hadn't gone far when the flashlight picked up the dark green of Paul's pickup. Laine swept the light around and we could see that the pickup was on its side, resting against a gnarled old juniper, the driver's side door uppermost. But where was Paul? He wasn't in the pickup. For one heart-stopping instant, I thought he must be under it. Laine probed with the flashlight and we both breathed easier when it was evident that Paul was not pinned underneath. Laine hoisted himself up and reached in through the broken window and turned off the pickup's headlights.

"He must have been thrown out when the pickup rolled," Laine said.

He started up the hill toward the road, with me right behind him. He swept the flashlight beam back and forth in wide arcs.

"There," I exclaimed. "There to the right a little." I had caught a glimpse of something light colored.

Laine directed the flashlight beam to the right and it picked up the white of the old man's fringe of hair. He was lying on his back, his arms flung wide, one leg twisted at a dreadfully unnatural angle.

"Oh, God," Laine cried.

We rushed to Paul and knelt beside him, one on either side. Laine shone the flashlight over the old man. There was blood on his face and on his shirt. His eyes flickered open and he looked from one of us to the other. His breathing was labored and shallow. He smiled at Laine.

"Laine." His voice was thin and weak, we had to lean close to hear him at all.

"I'm going for help, Grandpa. Marge will stay with you. Hang on, Grandpa."

Without waiting for my agreement, Laine handed me the flashlight and tore off up the hill. I heard the pickup start and saw the lights come on. Then it was gone and I was alone with Paul. The three-quarter moon had risen while we were examining the wrecked pickup so I turned the flashlight off. I ached to do something for Paul. The ground was cold and muddy, still frozen an inch or so below the surface so I took off my Pendleton shirt and put it over him. There was nothing else I could do.

Slowly, with great effort, Paul raised his hand to his head.

"Hurts," he said.

I caught his hand and held it gently, afraid he would cause himself more pain. I had to put my ear close to his mouth to hear him over the blare of the pickup horn.

"I know," I said. "Laine has gone for help. The doctor will be here soon to fix you up."

Paul gave me a look of mingled exasperation and understanding. "Too...late..." Even that took much of his remaining strength. He had to rest before he could speak again. Then he said, "Tell...Laine...lights..."

"Lights?" I was mystified. There were no lights. "I don't understand."

Paul made a great effort and said, "Lights...road..." His eyes closed.

The pickup horn was still blaring. It was the most maddening sound I had ever heard. It shrieked on and on, with no change in tone, no variation whatever. I wanted to go and rip the wires loose at the roots but I couldn't leave Paul. Then, under the sound of the horn, there was another sound. The sound as of someone slipping in the loose rocks on the slope, rocks rattling together. I raised my head to listen, frightened all at once.

"Who's there?" I called. I flicked the flashlight on and aimed it toward the sound. "Who are you?" I called again, louder.

There was a brittle, smashing sound, as of glass breaking on rocks. I froze, staring hard into the dark in the direction of the noise, knowing that such a sound then and there could bode no good. I tried to hold my breath so as to miss no further sound. Then I drew a deep breath and shook myself. My mind was playing tricks on me. It must be. The stress of finding Paul and being left alone with him in the dark and then the pickup horn blaring steadily, mindlessly, mercilessly -- all that must have combined to make me think I was hearing things that weren't there and couldn't be there. I looked down at Paul.

His eyes were open again, watching me. I wanted to cradle his head in my lap but did not dare move him. I badly wanted a blanket to put over him. "I'm going to see if there's a blanket or something in your pickup. I'll be back in a minute."

Paul blinked up at me. "No," he said.

46

"No blanket? But there may be something that would help a little. Even an empty feed bag would be something."

I gently laid his hand on his chest and stood up. I went to the pickup as quickly as I could and climbed up to look down into the cab. I already knew there was nothing in the pickup bed, all the miscellany that collects in the back of a pickup had fallen out as it rolled down the hill. I thought there might be something in the cab, though, maybe behind the seat. The hood was smashed so that I knew I couldn't open it to disconnect the horn but as I lowered myself into the cab, I thought it would be worth a try to kick the button in the middle of the steering wheel. I couldn't get a good, clear shot at it but I did manage to whack it a couple of times, not that it helped any. To my disappointment, though not to my surprise, there was nothing behind the seat but a few shotgun shells, some twenty-two casings, and a few juniper twigs and pine needles.

When I got back to Paul, I knelt beside him and spoke as softly as I could and still be heard over the horn.

"Paul? I couldn't find anything in your pickup to cover you with. Hold on, Laine will be here soon with help."

He spoke again, his speech slurred and faint. I

thought he said my name.

I leaned closer to him and took his hand.

"No...accident...," I thought he said. He paused. "Lights..."

I waited a few moments but he didn't say anything more just then. I didn't know if he had passed out or was too weak to talk. The moon, when next I noticed it, was surprisingly high. It illuminated the area well enough that I could see a whitened snag nearby. It looked ghostly and spooky in the moonlight. I wished I had some way of making a fire. The snag would be good firewood. But even supposing I could find some matches, there was nothing dry enough to use for kindling. My jeans were wet and muddy and I was chilled to the bone. I knew Paul was, too, and I prayed that help would come soon.

Paul tried to talk several times but I couldn't make out what he was saying. I hadn't looked at my watch when Laine left so I had no very clear idea of how long he had been gone. An hour and a half at least, I estimated. After what seemed a very long time, I realized that Paul was dead. I was never sure afterwards at exactly what point he had died. I continued to sit beside him, holding his hand until Laine drove up, the ambulance right behind him. Naturally, the ambulance driver had all the lights flashing and the siren screaming. On top of the pickup horn, it almost pushed me past the limit of my endurance. Fortunately, the driver switched it off before I did or said anything regrettable. It was so queer to see the long, low, limousine-style ambulance out in the middle of Rabbit Flat that I almost laughed aloud.

Laine jumped out of his pickup and came straight to where I sat with Paul. The two-man ambulance crew followed with a stretcher.

"We're too late. I figured we would be." One look at the attitudes of the two of us on the ground was enough to tell Laine that his grandfather was gone.

I stood up stiffly.

"You're not too late, Laine," I said. "If this had happened at the emergency room door, the doctors couldn't have saved him. He was hurt too badly."

Laine nodded. The ambulance attendants set the stretcher down beside Paul and one of them bent down to feel for a pulse. Not finding one, he put his stethoscope in his ears and listened for a heartbeat. He straightened up, looked at Laine and shook his head.

"I'm afraid he's gone, Laine," he said.

Laine nodded.

I was shivering in my cold, wet jeans and cotton shirt. It had been marginally warmer sitting in the mud. At least part of me had been protected from the cold breeze. The second ambulance attendant brought the blanket from the stretcher and put it around my shoulders. The gesture of kindness caused me to humiliate myself by bursting into tears.

"Thank you," I said. "I'm sorry. I'm acting like a baby. I'm sorry."

The attendant patted my shoulder and turned back to help his partner lift Paul's body onto the stretcher.

Laine put his arm around my shoulders. "It's okay, Marge. I understand. Come and get in the pickup where it's warm."

I allowed him to lead me up the hill to his pickup. He opened the door and I climbed in, pulling the blanket closely around me. Laine got in and started the motor so I would have heat. Then he got some tools out of the back of his pickup and went down to his grandfather's. He pried the hood up and the horn stopped its blaring. The relief was stupendous. I watched him come back up the hill and stop to speak to the men at the back of the ambulance.

After they closed the door, the three men stood at the edge of the road and looked at the wrecked pickup and the marks on the shoulder of the road where it had gone over. I watched them gesticulating as they discussed it. They seemed to be puzzled about something. Finally, they climbed into their respective vehicles and got turned around and headed back toward Bend. I had stopped crying by then but I was still shivering. I thought it was entirely possible that I would never again be really warm.

"We'll stop at the house and get you a shot of something to warm you up," Laine said. "Brandy or Four Roses or something."

"I'm okay," I said. "Please don't stop. I can't meet people like this."

"You want to go straight to the motel?"

"Yes, please. I need a hot shower more than anything else."

"Your car is at the house."

"Oh, that's right. Well, then, drop me off at my car."

Laine glanced over at me. "You're in no state of mind to drive. I'll take you in to Bend and bring your car in tomorrow. Brad can follow me and pick me up."

"I can drive. I'm okay."

Laine shot me a look but didn't say anything for another mile or two.

"Dr. Harris -- that was Dr. Harris with the stethoscope back there -- said the same thing you did. That Grandpa was hurt too bad; no one could have saved him." Laine glanced at me and put his hand over mine, where it was resting on the seat between us. "I want to thank you for what you did. Staying with him and all. I know it wasn't easy for you."

"I just felt so helpless. I wanted to do something for him but there was nothing I could do. I'm so sorry, Laine. He was such a fine man."

Laine nodded. I was warm enough by then to stop shivering but I wouldn't be really warm all through until I got out of my wet jeans.

"What were you and Dr. Harris and that other guy talking about?" I asked.

"What? When?"

"When you were standing there. Just before we started back to town."

"Oh. We were looking at the tracks the pickup made going off the road. There weren't any skid marks in the mud, no sign that he'd tried to stop before he went over."

"That seems strange."

Laine nodded. "Unless he passed out and lost control."

I frowned, thinking about the scene as I'd first seen it. "Maybe. But he was conscious when we got there."

"He was?" Laine was surprised.

"At least part of the time he was."

"How could you tell?"

"Well, he spoke. He was trying to tell me something. He tried several times but he was too weak to get it all out. I couldn't really understand. He wanted me to tell you something."

"Can you remember what he said at all?"

"He said your name and then, 'lights.' Something about lights. He said that twice. And he said something about the road. But I couldn't tell what he meant. It didn't make any sense to me. Only he seemed kind of urgent about it."

"Lights and the road. But he was the only one out there, there weren't any other lights."

"I didn't notice if there were any other tracks. Did you?" I asked.

Laine shook his head. "I didn't really look, though."

I shivered, not with cold but with remembered fear. "Laine, there might have been someone else out there. I thought I heard someone in the rocks. And there was a sound as if someone had dropped a water jug or something and broke it."

"Did you see anyone?"

"No. I only heard some noises. And with the horn blowing like that, I couldn't even be sure of that. I mean, it doesn't make sense. If there'd been anyone there, they'd have come to see what was the matter."

"So you'd think."

We were quiet until we got out to the highway and I realized that Laine was taking me back to the motel instead of to my car.

"Laine," I exclaimed. "There's no need to take me clear in to Bend. Just take me to my car and I'll drive back."

He turned and smiled at me. "Marge, let me do this much. You've been through an awful time and I need to do something for you, even if it's just to take you home."

It finally dawned on me that Laine was very near tears himself, with grief and strain. And while my ordeal was over, his was just beginning. He still had to go home and tell Ricki and his relatives about Paul's death. I decided to be generous.

"All right. I can get my car tomorrow."

"Call the house when you're ready and I'll come get you."

"Okay. Thanks."

I left the blanket in the pickup when I got out at my motel room door. I remembered to take my purse. We exchanged goodnights and Laine waited until I had unlocked the door and gone inside before driving away. I flipped the lights on and locked the door then peeled off those awful clothes and got under the hot shower. It was heavenly.

Chapter 4

I was putting pincurls in my wet hair when there was a knock on the door. I couldn't imagine who it could be. It wasn't all that late, only about ten o'clock, but I didn't know anyone in Bend except the Crittendens. Thinking it might be Laine coming back for some reason, I opened the door. To my utter astonishment, a young woman was standing there with a large paper bag. She was a pretty woman, one of those diminutive blonds with blue eyes and dimples. At that moment the blue eyes were full of somber sympathy. She smiled sadly.

"Hi," she said. "I'm Audrey Wells. I'm a friend of Laine Crittenden's. He told me what happened tonight and asked me to come over and bring you something to eat. And drink."

My astonishment finally gave way to good manners. I stepped back and held the door open, "Come in. Let me take that."

She handed me the paper bag and I set it on the

little round table in the corner of the room. She closed the door and I invited her to sit down. There were three chairs in the room and she laid her coat on the bed and chose to sit in one of the two chairs beside the table. I sat in the other and wondered what on earth I was to say to her. Fortunately, she didn't seem to notice my awkwardness. She opened the bag and began to take things out.

"I hope you like vegetable beef soup. It was the only kind I had. Laine suggested coffee because you'd nearly frozen to death out there but I thought hot chocolate would be better this time of night. And there's a banana and some crackers and an Almond Joy."

As she talked, she took things out of the bag, finishing with a paper plate, a couple of paper cups, a bowl, a spoon, and some paper napkins.

"You take my breath away," I said. "All this for a total stranger."

She smiled and patted my hand. "Any friend of Laine's is a friend of mine. Here, why don't you start with some hot chocolate?"

Miss Wells tipped the thermos back and forth to mix the milk and chocolate then poured a cup for me.

"Please," I said. "Join me, this is all too much."

She smiled, forgetting to be somber and poured a

second cup.

"I hope it's hot enough. I kind of hurried because I wanted to get here before you got in bed. Laine said you were pretty well beat." She reached into the bag again and took out a tiny bottle of creme de cacao. "Put this in your hot chocolate, it'll help you relax."

"Great Scott, what all do you have in that bag?" I exclaimed.

Miss Wells laughed. "That's all. My mom and dad went to Reno for New Year's and brought back some of these little bottles. Cute, aren't they? Here, let me have your cup."

"Only if you'll put half of it in your cup. I'm so tired I'm sure to fall asleep the instant my head touches the pillow."

"Okay, it's a deal."

She poured the liqueur into our cups and we sipped. It was delicious -- so warm and comforting.

"How about some soup?" She asked, reaching for the second thermos.

I shook my head. "I couldn't eat now. I'm too...I don't know, keyed up? Too emotionally engaged."

"I know how you feel. In a turmoil." She got up and went into the bathroom, coming back with my bobby pins and a comb. "You drink your hot chocolate and I'll finish your pincurls."

"Oh, I'd forgotten all about my hair. I must look a

fright." I was embarrassed but I hadn't been expecting company.

"After what you've been through, no one expects you to look as if you'd just stepped out of a bandbox. Whatever a bandbox is."

I smiled. "I have always wondered what a bandbox is. I've always kind of pictured it as a hat box of some kind."

I bowed to the inevitable and sipped my hot chocolate while Miss Wells deftly wrapped my hair around her finger and fastened it with bobby pins. We chatted of Laine, the Crittendens, and the beauties of central Oregon. I told her about Paul's death. She seemed distressed for Laine and grieved for Paul, as well. By the time we had finished the hot chocolate, we were on a first name basis and I found that I liked her very much. I started to put things back into the paper bag.

"No, don't pack up. I'm going to leave everything here except this empty thermos. You may get hungry later on," she said, putting on her coat.

"I'll leave the other thermos with Laine tomorrow," I said. "My car is out there and I'll have to go out and get it."

"That'll be fine. Good night, Marge. Hope I'll see you again soon."

"Good night, Audrey. Thank you for everything."

She smiled and went out to her car. I watched from the doorway until she got in and drove away. I locked the door and turned off the light. Ten seconds later I was in bed. Contrary to my expectations, I did not sleep immediately. I thought about Paul lying there in the mud, cold and dying, with that horrible horn blaring without cessation. There was nothing I could have done to help him but that did not completely assuage the guilt feelings. It just seemed all wrong that he was dead and I was here, safe and warm, quiet and physically comfortable.

When I finally fell asleep, my dreams were filled with images of death and cold. I seemed to hear the pickup horn blowing as a sort of theme song. I struggled to waken from the dreams only to fall back into them again. It was about six when I gave up on sleeping and got up and put my robe on. I wished for some coffee or tea as I sat at the window and watched the Deschutes make its unruly way north. It was somehow soothing to my rumpled feelings to watch the river roil and froth over the boulders.

The need for sustenance and human contact got me moving at last. I put on a skirt and sweater and a pair of black flats. My hair combed out of its pincurls just as if I hadn't passed a harrowing night. A touch of lipstick and I was ready. I slipped on my coat and picked up my purse, not bothering with gloves. There was a coffee shop down the street a couple of blocks. There weren't many people out and about yet that early on a Sunday morning, just a couple of cowboys at the lunch counter and a sleepy little family in one of the booths. The waitress, who looked like a high school girl in her yellow and white uniform and bobby sox, took my order for coffee and a short stack of pancakes with a side of bacon. The coffee was good and I enjoyed my breakfast. I was just sipping my third cup of coffee when, to my intense amazement, Laine Crittenden came in, spotted me and sat down in the booth opposite me. He looked, not to put too fine a point on it, like hell.

"Good morning," he said, with a tired smile.

"Good morning. Did you get any sleep at all last night?"

"Not a lot. How about you?"

"It wasn't a really restful night." I looked for the waitress to ask her for coffee for Laine but she was already on her way over with a cup and saucer and the coffee pot.

"Hi, Mr. Crittenden," she said, with a brilliant smile.

"Hi, Ellen."

She poured a cup of coffee for him and refilled my cup. She peered into the cream pitcher but it was still full.

"What would you like besides coffee?" she asked.

"Nothing. I've already had my breakfast."

She flashed him another brilliant smile, "Let me know if you change your mind."

Laine nodded at her. "I will. Thanks."

She went back to her counter then and Laine tested the heat of his coffee. Finding it a bit too hot for comfort, he set the cup in its saucer.

"Marge, did anything strike you as strange about Grandpa's accident last night?"

I was too surprised to answer for a couple of seconds. "No, not really."

He pounced on the ambiguity of my answer. "So you did feel that something wasn't right. What?"

I squirmed uncomfortably. "I don't know exactly. It wasn't anything really definite. Maybe that he was trying so hard to get a message to you. Or maybe the noises I thought I heard."

"Will you go out there with me this morning? I want to look it over by daylight."

I didn't want to go. I wanted to forget the whole business just as soon as I could. But I couldn't walk away from the pain in Laine's face. Whether I wanted to be or not, I was part of the events of last night and I had an obligation to help if I could.

"Okay," I said. "Now?"

"Yes, if you're finished."

"I'm fine. Have you really had breakfast? If you haven't, you should eat something now. I expect you didn't eat dinner last night, either."

Laine shook his head. "I couldn't swallow anything."

We stood up and I put my coat on. He reached in his pocket but I went quickly over to the cash register and paid Ellen, adding a tip that was a tad more than sufficient.

As we pulled away from the curb, I thanked him for sending Audrey over with food and hot chocolate.

"Audrey and I are old friends. She knows I'd do anything for her. She and Grandpa were buddies, too. In fact, he financed her when she went to Portland to beauty school."

"She's very nice, I liked her a lot."

"She liked you, too." He glanced at me and saw the surprise on my face.

"We talked on the phone this morning."

Laine told me a little more about his family on the way out to Rabbit Flat. His father's second wife was considerably younger than he. She had two teen-age daughters from an earlier marriage. Together they had produced a son and a daughter: Ray was six and Molly was four.

"I'll bet that seems a little strange, having a

brother and sister young enough to be your own children," I said.

"Well, I'd have had to hustle some. But yes, it does seem a little strange. They're great little kids, though."

"Do you see them often?"

"No. Dad's business keeps him pretty well tied to the Rogue River Valley. He has a little Cessna, though, and he flies over every now and then. He doesn't often bring Agnes and the kids."

"You have just the two aunts?" I asked.

"On Dad's side of the family, yes, and some cousins. Aunt Elmyra -- she's the one who came in yesterday -- is older than Dad and Aunt Lorena is younger. Aunt Elmyra and Uncle Leroy brought their son, Brad, with them, and Brad's girlfriend."

"You don't care much for that branch of the family?"

"Oh, they're all right. Brad's kind of a pain. He's never settled down to do anything. Just bums around, acting rich."

"Acting rich? I have always understood that the Crittendens are rich."

Laine gave me a smile that seemed to be compounded of embarrassment, apology, and irritation.

"Grandpa was rich," he said. "He shared with his

63

kids but none of them are what you could actually call rich. Dad is pretty well off. He flies his own plane and has a nice house and drives a Cadillac convertible. But Aunt Elmyra and Aunt Lorena -- well, they have enough but not a lot extra."

"I see." I was getting a picture of the Crittenden family that I didn't much like. On the other hand, I knew I ought to be careful not to form any opinions at second hand. My dad had always told us that people ought to do their own thinking.

"Where does your other aunt live? Lorena."

"Reno. Uncle Elwood has an air taxi service and runs a flying school. He taught my dad to fly."

"You don't fly?"

Laine shook his head. "I've never been interested in it. I've flown commercially a few times and I've been up with Dad but I have no desire to be a pilot."

"I've never been up in a plane. I'm not sure if I'd like it or not."

"It's interesting if you're low enough to see things but once the plane is so high that all you can see is clouds, it's just boring."

The mention of clouds reminded me of how the Miller twins had gotten interested in weather when I had incautiously assigned them a report on the subject. I told Laine about it and he was highly amused by the ensuing difficulties I became embroiled in as a result.

"You can't keep up with a couple of fifth grade girls?" he asked incredulously.

I longed to lock him in a schoolroom with them for a week. It would be such a relief to see someone besides myself pilloried by their combined intelligences.

"These are not just your ordinary fifth graders," I said darkly.

"Evidently not. Still, they are only little girls, of, what? Ten or eleven?"

"They are eleven. They'll be twelve sometime in the middle of June. I will have them in my schoolroom for three more years. It isn't a happy thought."

Laine laughed. "Come on, they can't be as bad as all that."

"They invented a language," I told him. "They call it Quoskeen. It has an extensive vocabulary, a complete set of grammatical rules, and is both written and spoken. The other children find it even more exasperating than I do."

Laine looked at me to see if I was telling him a tall tale but my expression appeared to convince him that this was not of the Paul Bunyan order of stories. He looked uncertain as to whether to laugh or commiserate.

"How do you know it has a complete grammar? Have they taught you this language?"

"No, but they correct each other occasionally. Besides, I know Dottie and Debbie. They are very thorough in everything they undertake. It's gotten so I hate to assign them reports because I know I'll have to do a lot of studying before I can grade them."

"Marge, you are fibbing to me." I opened my mouth to deny it but he swept on. "Not about the twins but about your feelings toward them. Far from being exasperated, you are extremely pleased and delighted. Admit it, now."

I grinned at him. "All right, you nailed me. They are the most interesting pair of juveniles that I have ever encountered. Of course, I'm just at the beginning of my teaching career. For all I know, they are the norm and the other children are the exceptions. But Dottie and Debbie are certainly both a joy and a terror to teach."

We talked about school the rest of the way out to Rabbit Flat, comparing our own school days, which had been roughly contemporaneous. Laine was a couple of years older than I and, while I had gone to the Heppner Grade School all eight years, he had gone to six different grade schools, some rural, some town. He hadn't liked all the moving around and always having to make new friends but he felt it might have given him a broader outlook than if he'd stayed in one place.

I thought it over and concluded that he was probably right. Maybe, I thought, my own viewpoint needed broadening. I had never traveled much, being quite happy with home, but maybe it would be a good thing if I took a few trips. Maybe even move away from Camp Five and get a job in the city somewhere. I shuddered. Not that. Surely, I didn't need broadening as much as that.

While I was mentally retreating back to my comfortable schoolroom in Camp Five, Laine parked the pickup near where Paul's pickup had gone over the bank. He was careful not to disturb the tracks from the night before.

Realizing that my concentration on thoughts of travel were a retreat from thinking about Paul's death, I gave myself a mental yank and braced myself for the onslaught of emotions. It's a good thing I did or I might have burst into tears at the sight of Paul's pickup on its side under the juniper tree. I was shaking a little from suppressed feelings when I climbed out of the pickup. Laine also got out and we stood at the edge of the road, looking at the churned up mud where I'd sat so long the night before, first with Paul and then with his body.

We started slowly forward, looking at the ground,

trying to decipher the tangle of tire tracks and footprints. We had gotten as far as where the ambulance had stopped when we heard a car coming.

"Damn," Laine exclaimed. "Who the hell is that?"

"Somebody in a hurry," I said.

"Two somebodies; there are two cars. Maybe I can head them off. I don't want any traffic over this until I have a chance to sort it out."

He stepped into the middle of the road. In a couple of minutes, the pink Olds came around the turn, followed by a Deschutes County Sheriff's Department car. Paul's cousin Brad was driving the civilian car. Laine waved to Brad to stop but had to jump out of the way when he saw that Brad wasn't braking.

Chapter Five

Indignantly, I watched as Brad barreled past us, then slammed on his brakes, skidded to a stop and turned around, then stopped right in the middle of the road. The two deputies had pulled over behind Laine's pickup. They got out and walked over to us. Brad also got out and came over.

"What the hell's the matter with you, Brad?" Laine demanded angrily.

Brad grinned. "Hey, what are you so mad about? I brought the cops. They said they need to see the scene of the accident."

Laine gave his cousin a withering look, then turned to the deputies. Making an effort to set aside his anger, he shook hands with them and introduced me.

"Marge, this is Deputy Sheriff Perce Culverton and Deputy Mac McIntosh. Marge O'Connor."

The deputies nodded at me and I bobbed my head at them.

Deputy Culverton was a medium kind of guy, medium height, medium coloring, medium weight. If his I.Q. was better than medium, it would be very easy to underestimate him. Deputy McIntosh was more like a pear than an apple. He had narrow shoulders but wide hips. His demeanor was very serious, very much on the job. Both deputies were taking in the attitudes of Laine and Brad.

Laine gave them a brief outline of what we'd found last night and they looked over the tracks on the road -- what Brad's silliness hadn't obliterated. Deputy McIntosh wrote on a clipboard and sketched in a diagram of the scene.

"So he was still alive when you got here?" Deputy Culverton asked.

"Yeah. As soon as we found him -- Marge found him -- I lit out to call the ambulance. Marge stayed here with Grandpa."

Both deputies looked at me skeptically.

"You weren't afraid to be left alone with the deceased, ma'am?" Deputy Culverton clearly didn't know what to make of me.

"No, of course not. Afraid of what? Besides, he wasn't deceased when Laine left." I wondered what on earth he was getting at, what he expected me to say.

"How did you know he was still alive? Did he

talk to you?"

"I knew he was alive because his eyes were open and he watched Laine and me. And he was breathing, kind of quick and shallow."

Laine corroborated that. "He was alive. He was breathing and watching us. I could see he was badly hurt, though."

Deputy Culverton appeared to cogitate on that.

"Didn't he say anything?" Brad asked eagerly. "Anything at all?"

Both deputies scowled at him.

"I'll ask the questions, Mr. Boggs," Deputy Culverton said.

"Sorry." Brad didn't look sorry. There was a kind of gleeful excitement behind his effort to appear calm and mournful.

Deputy Culverton asked a couple of questions about the time Laine and I arrived there last night and if we'd seen anything likely to help in determining the cause of the accident. After that, I guess he felt he could ask without seeming to be taking hints from civilians, so he asked if Paul had said anything before he died.

"Not really," I said. "Just disconnected words. I could barely hear him, his voice was so weak and low.

"But you could make out some words?" Deputy

Culverton persisted.

"He said 'lights' a couple of times. And he said Laine's name." I struggled to remember exactly what Paul's words had been. "Oh, yes, when I told him Laine had gone for the doctor, he said it was too late. I guess he knew how badly he was hurt."

The deputy nodded. "What construction did you put on the word 'lights' when deceased said it?"

"None," I said. "There didn't seem to be any relevancy at all. Unless he meant that he wrecked because the light was bad and he'd run off the road because of it. It must have been dark or nearly dark when he had the accident."

The two deputies exchanged nods.

"You folks wait here, please. Deputy McIntosh and I will go over the ground and make some measurements."

We stood and watched as the deputies followed Paul's tire tracks from the road to the shallow borrow pit. Paul must have been going at a pretty good clip because the pickup had rolled on down the hill until the juniper stopped it. Of course, the camber of the road and the borrow pit below it would have functioned like a ramp for the near front tire and would have launched the pickup upwards.

"Grandpa didn't put on his brakes at all," Brad said, examining the tracks at the edge of the road.

"Maybe he fell asleep or had a stroke or something."

"Shut up," Laine snarled.

"Oh, dry up," Brad snarled back at him. "Just because you were his favorite, you think the rest of us don't count. But he was my grandpa just as much as he was yours." A pleased smile broke out on his face. "And I'll bet my share of the money will be just as big as yours, too."

Laine lost his temper in earnest then. He took two long strides, which brought him nearly toe to toe with Brad. His right arm shot out and he landed a lovely punch right square on Brad's nose. I have never seen anything to equal the wrathful surprise on Brad's face as blood streamed out of his nose and the pain registered. He recovered himself instantly and struck back with what Laine afterwards told me was meant to be a right to the jaw, although he dodged and the blow merely brushed by him.

They squared off and began to hammer at one another in earnest. Maybe I should have tried to stop them, shouted for the deputies or something. I did nothing. For one thing, I needed a release for my feelings just as much as they did and I thought Laine could take Brad. For another, Lyle Allston and Ray Troupe, two of my pupils, fought regularly out on the playground and I knew how easy it was for a peace-maker to catch a painful punch. Lots more painful from these guys than from a couple of twelve-year-olds. And, too, I didn't think it was likely that they'd do each other any lasting damage.

The two deputies didn't share my laissez faire attitude. They came boiling up the hill, grim and purposeful. Deputy McIntosh dropped his clipboard and pen on the hood of Brad's car and waded into the battle with Deputy Culverton. Each deputy grabbed a disputant, shouting things like "hold it, now," and "here, now, what's all this?" It didn't take long to separate them and the four men stood and panted, glaring at one another.

Brad jerked his arm free of Deputy Culverton and flounced into his car. He slammed the door and started it up. I was rather glad that it was muddy rather than dusty when he gunned the motor and spun out. At that, he threw quite a lot of mud but it missed us for the most part. The deputy's clipboard fell off the hood as Brad fishtailed past. We never did find the pen.

When Brad was around the corner, out of sight, the two deputies turned to Laine.

"What was that all about?" Deputy Culverton asked.

"Nothing," Laine said. "Brad just said something that teed me off."

"Evidently," the deputy agreed, dryly.

Deputy McIntosh retrieved his clipboard and dislodged the biggest chunks of mud. "Do any of you have a pen or pencil I can borrow?" he asked.

"I think I have one in my purse," I said and started toward the pickup.

"Miss O'Connor's a schoolmarm," Laine said.

"Don't bother, ma'am," Deputy Culverton said. "I have one."

He opened the squad car door and leaned in, coming back out with a pen that he handed to his sidekick. Deputy McIntosh wrote a few words or figures on the sketch of the accident scene and stood, comparing the sketch to the actual scene.

"There'll have to be an autopsy, Laine," Deputy Culverton said.

Laine nodded. "I figured there'd have to be."

"We'll notify the mortuary when the body can be released, if you'll let us know which one."

"Tibbett's. We've always used them."

The deputy nodded. "Mac, you got everything down?"

Deputy McIntosh came over to us. "Yeah. It's kind of muddy but I'll copy it over back at the office."

"All right. Laine, you know how bad we feel over this. Your granddad was a fine man, well-liked and respected."

"Thanks."

Laine shook hands with both deputies again and they tipped their hats to me. I nodded at them and they got in the squad car and drove away.

"Sorry about that, Marge," Laine said. "Fighting in front of you like that."

"It's okay. I understand. Brad was being rather irritating."

"That's an understatement."

As he talked, Laine walked up the road, past the place where Paul's pickup had gone over. I couldn't see much of anything after that except the mess Brad had made when he'd made his spectacular skidding stop and turn and then peeled out. There were some tracks farther on but not many. I couldn't tell for sure, but they looked to me to be the ones Paul had made going to check the windmill and coming back. There were no tracks as of brakes suddenly slammed on, as one would expect if Paul had met another vehicle. All the tracks went right down the middle of the road. I said so to Laine.

"Well, I'm no tracker, but that's how it looks to me, too. I just can't see any reason for Grandpa to have gone off the road like that."

We walked down to Paul's pickup and Laine looked back at the spot where his grandfather had lain dying the night before. He scanned the area back and forth and his gaze stopped at a tumble of rocks near the road, about thirty yards from where I'd sat with Paul. They had evidently been dislodged when the road was made and had been left where they'd fallen.

"That must be where the noise I heard came from," I said. "Something walking on the rocks and slipping."

"Like what?"

"I don't know. Not a deer. They can see well enough at night to avoid rocks like that. A coyote, maybe."

Laine looked skeptical. "Maybe. A porcupine? Skunk?"

"I wouldn't think they'd be heavy enough to move the rocks when they walk. It sounded like -- I don't know -- something heavy walking on the loose rocks. Like a bear."

Laine laughed shortly. "A bear? Down this far? It's been years since anyone's seen a bear around here except 'way up in the mountains."

"I know. I didn't mean I thought it was a bear, just something big and heavy, like a bear."

Laine was serious again. "Are you trying not to say you thought it was a man, Marge?"

I was momentarily startled, then I realized that was precisely what I had thought and didn't want to think.

"I guess so," I said. "And then there was the other sound, too. Like something tinny had been dropped. I know at the time it made me think of a gas lantern."

"Like metal and glass falling and the glass breaking?"

"Something like that. I decided it was my nerves playing tricks on me. And that's probably what it was."

"Probably."

"Well, of course," I said impatiently. "If there'd been anyone there, any person, they would have come to see if they could help. Naturally."

Laine gave me a look, gauging my gullibility or naiveté or something.

"Don't look at me like that, Laine."

"Okay, okay," he said pacifically.

He walked over to the rocks and scouted around them, looking for footprints of some kind, I guessed.

"Find anything?" I asked, coming up with him.

"No. If there was someone or something here last night, these cow tracks have obliterated them."

"Lights," I said thoughtfully. "Paul said 'lights' a couple of times. Maybe whoever it was did use a light."

Laine was poking around in the rocks. He stooped over and picked something up. I saw it glint in the sunlight. He held it out to me. I took it and looked at it in some puzzlement. It was a tiny shard of glass. I looked at him and our eyes locked. There was some meaning here that we couldn't comprehend.

We walked back to the pickup and Laine placed the glass shard in the casing of a thirty-ought-six round.

"Put this in your purse, would you?" he asked.

"Sure."

I was surprised but I wrapped it in a clean tissue and tucked it in a corner at the bottom of my handbag. I couldn't imagine what he wanted it for. He nodded at the small tools and miscellaneous junk that had fallen out of Paul's pickup on its trip down the hill.

"I might as well pick that up. No sense in leaving it out here."

"I'll help."

Laine unearthed an empty feed sack from the back of his pickup and handed it to me. For himself he found a large galvanized bucket with a couple of big dents in it. I've often wondered on what system men base their pickup bed collections. Usefulness doesn't seem to be the primary criteria. Uncle Miles keeps everything from jumper cables and tire irons and jacks to rusty saws with broken teeth and axe heads with broken handles in his. And the jack doesn't necessarily fit the rig it's in, as my cousins and I found out one day when we were over in the Ochoco National Forest, about twenty miles from civilization, and had a flat tire. Phil had to walk about five miles before he caught a ride into Prineville.

If I had been able to laugh at anything in connection with Paul's death, I could have laughed at the uselessness of most of the stuff Laine and I picked up. Rusty horse shoes, a broken come-along, coils of wire of various kinds in various stages of dilapidation (but no doubt they would come in handy some day for something), one of a pair of gloves. Of course, there were useful tools, too. Laine found a brand-new fencing tool that still had the price tag on it and there were a number of hammers and screwdrivers of different kinds and uses.

When we had picked up everything we could find, we took it back to the road and Laine heaved the bucket and the sack into the back of his pickup. I suspected that it would meld into the mass of oddments that he had already collected and would still be there when he traded the pickup off, whether that took place in a few months or a few years.

We got into the cab and Laine started the motor.

"I'll have to call Ron Metzler and get him to come

out and tow Grandpa's pickup in."

"You don't have to leave it here for the insurance people to look at?"

Laine shook his head. "They can check it out at Metzler's. He has a wrecking yard and he can take it there. I can't imagine that the insurance people wouldn't total it out. It's pretty old. I don't know what Blue Book would be on it but probably not more than four or five hundred dollars."

I was mildly surprised when Laine drove on instead of turning around and heading back to the ranch house. He glanced over at me and smiled fleetingly.

"I hope you don't mind, Marge. I just want to check out that windmill."

I didn't mind and told him so. I don't know what he expected or hoped to find at the windmill and his face didn't give me any indication when we saw that the mill was turning lazily in the light breeze. When he pulled up and stopped we saw that the stock tank was full. The mud was all churned up around the tank where the cattle had come to drink.

Laine and I got out of the pickup and walked around the windmill and water tank, keeping a good distance from the worst of the churned up mud, trying to see any footprints or tire prints that could possibly relate to last night. But neither of us knew

81

all that much about tracking. I can tell a deer's hoof print from a duck's foot print but that's about as far as I can go.

"I can't see any boot prints," I told Laine when we'd come back to our starting point. "But I don't know much about tracking. How about you?"

"Nope twice." He took off his hat and ran a hand over his hair, then put the hat back on. "I can't see any boot prints and I don't know much about tracking, either. I can see some tire tracks here and there but I can't put my hand on them and tell how old they are."

I smiled at that. "You mean like in the movies? I don't know how such nonsense gets started."

"I do." Laine grinned at me. "Someone reads a western novel and it tells how the hero felt the 'spoor' and pronounced the quarry an hour and a half ahead. The people who write for the movies think spoor means foot prints, not knowing that it includes more tangible tracks -- for instance, cow pies or road apples. The novel writers of bygone days being too genteel, of course, to specify what kind of spoor could be expected to cool with age."

I laughed. "I expect that's how it got started and now it's firmly entrenched in the mythology of the old west. Anything else you want to look at while we're here?"

Laine shook his head and we got back in the cab and he started back toward the house. As we passed the site of the accident, we both looked at Paul's pickup, lying wounded and forlorn on its side.

"What did you expect to see at the windmill, Laine?" I asked.

"I don't know. I just wanted to see if there was anything unusual out there. I thought maybe he'd met someone who had upset him."

"I see. Trying to account for the accident."

"Yes. Grandpa was old but he wasn't feeble. His reflexes were slowing down but he could still drive all right. He could see all right, too. I don't suppose his sight was as good as when he was sixty or even eighty, but he could see well enough to drive, even at night."

"I wish I knew what he was trying to tell me last night. I tried to make it out but he wasn't speaking in sentences, you know. He was just speaking the most important words, hoping, I guess, that I could put them in context and tell what he meant."

"Don't worry about it, Marge. It probably wasn't important and, even if it was, there's nothing we can do about it now."

I agreed with Laine but I couldn't help wishing I'd been able to understand Paul. He had been very urgent about it, whatever it was. I sent up a little silent prayer for him and for his family.

The family was very much in evidence when we pulled into the parking area between the house and the barn. Elmyra and Leroy Boggs, with Brad and his girlfriend, were standing near the hood of a new dark green Studebaker, watching four people get out of it, all of whom were dressed in black. The driver was a middle-aged woman with improbably red hair and a sour expression; the front seat passenger was a man of about the same vintage with lots of wavy brown hair. The other passengers were a young woman who wore her curly brown hair shoulder length and a rosy-cheeked young man who looked impossibly cherubic.

"Oh, lord," Laine groaned. "There's Aunt Lorena with her family, or part of it. I didn't know she was coming so soon."

"Why? Does she live far away?"

Laine grimaced as he brought the pickup to a stop and turned off the motor.

"Not nearly far enough," he said wryly. "She lives in Kansas. They must have flown to have gotten here so soon. That's her daughter Janet with her and Janet's husband. I forget his name."

The assorted sisters, cousins, and in-laws had finished the requisite hugging and hand-shaking, which had looked a little perfunctory to me, and were

84

all looking in our direction.

"Listen," Laine said, "if you don't want to meet this mob, you don't need to. I'll walk you to your car and you can make your get-away while I fight a rear-guard action."

"It's okay. I'd like to meet them. Then I will make my excuses and go. I'll come back in a week or two and get everything settled about Lotsa Spots. I do want to buy her but you won't want to be bothered with that now."

"I'd much rather be bothered by you than them."

Chapter 6

The closer we got to the group by the Studebaker, the more clearly I saw what Laine meant. The two older women were all but glowering, while the men looked impatient, and the younger quartet looked downright hostile. Laine appeared to notice nothing amiss in their various expressions but smiled at them blandly as he introduced me. No one offered to shake my hand and only Janet Eddingfield offered Laine any show of affection. She smiled at him and hugged him briefly.

"Hi, Laine," Janet said. Her expression became sad. "I'm sorry it's not a happier occasion but I'm glad to see you. How have you been?"

"All right. How about you? The kids okay?"

"They're fine. Billie's going to kindergarten now and she's all excited about it. Stevie can't understand why he can't go to 'kinnygarn', too, and Chloe has just started walking." She smiled sheepishly, shooting a glance around the circle. "I brought pictures to show you."

"Later, Janet," Elmyra said curtly. "Right now we have a lot to discuss. I'm sure Miss O'Connor will excuse us."

"Yes, of course." I said, in my best brisk, schoolmarm manner. "I'll leave you to it. I'm so sorry about Paul's death. Nice to have met you all." I gave them a rather wintry smile and turned to Laine. "I'll be in touch about Spot in a couple of weeks, if that's okay."

"That'll be fine," he said.

He walked me to my car.

"I'd invite you to lunch only I like you too much to subject you to the company of my revered aunts and their stuffed-shirt husbands."

"Families can be pretty awful at times like this; I hope you don't have a bad time with them. If I can do anything, let me know. I don't have a phone but my address is just Camp Five, Kinzua. Tell Mrs. Fenton that I'm sorry I didn't get a chance to say goodbye."

"All right. Have a safe trip home."

"I will."

I got in my car and started it. Laine turned to walk away but he had only gone a couple of steps when a thought occurred to me and I rolled my window down and called him back. The others had started for the house but most of them glanced back when they heard me. Elmyra shooed them on up the steps and inside.

"Laine, where do Janet and her husband live?"

He looked surprised. "They have a wheat ranch out in eastern Montana, near a little town called Vida. Why?"

"I just wondered how they got here so fast."

Laine looked thoughtful. "Yeah, I was kind of wondering that myself. Uncle El is an assistant warden or whatever they're called at Leavenworth. They couldn't have gotten here in this time even if they'd driven night and day. Maybe they flew. There's a commercial airport at Redmond."

"Maybe. But the license plate on their car is a Kansas one."

He shot a startled look at the car and, seeing the Kansas plate, nodded.

"That calls for an explanation, I think."

"I'm sorry," I said and meant it. I was sorry to plant doubts in his mind about his relatives and sorry that he was going to have a bad time sorting it all out. I thought his suspicions matched mine, although we were both fighting shy of naming them directly, as if that would reinforce them and give them substance.

Laine stood looking after me as I drove away. I waved and he waved back, then the shrubbery around the house blocked our view of each other and I headed back to Bend. It wasn't noon yet when I collected my suitcase at the motel and paid my bill. I debated whether to have lunch before I hit the road or eat somewhere along the line. There weren't a lot of choices. I could go back through Prineville and Mitchell or up through Madras and Antelope and Fossil. I had my gas tank filled at a Texaco service station and thought about it while the attendant checked my oil and water and tires. Deciding to go the quickest way, I went out past the radio station toward Prineville.

By the time I got there, I was hungry so I stopped at a little cafe on the main drag and ate a ham sandwich with cole slaw. I don't know what the cook put in her cole slaw but it was the best I've ever eaten. I paid the waitress for the bottle and took my strawberry soda with me. It was a nice drive home -- I always enjoyed the Painted Hills out of Mitchell and the play of light and cloud shadow over the landscape. As I wound down the mountain from Mitchell to the John Day River, I thought about Laine and Audrey. I wondered just how close the friendship between them was. It must be pretty darn close for him to go to her as he did the night before to ask her to take food and comfort to me. For all I knew they might be engaged and if so, more power to them. I liked them both and wished them well.

From there my thoughts turned to Paul and his accident. It felt less and less accidental. If I really had heard someone moving in the rocks last night and the breaking of glass, there was every possibility that Paul had been murdered. I had been trying very hard for a night and most of a day to push the word murder back, out of sight and out of mind. It wasn't working, though. I fought with myself clear to the junction of the company road with the highway. As I turned from the pavement onto the gravel, I said the word aloud.

"Murder." In itself, not an ugly word at all. Similar to verdure, which is a lovely word in both sound and concept. But the concept of murder is so ugly that the words used to express it are also ugly. I realized I was thinking about language in order to postpone thinking about Paul's death so I applied some mental discipline and began to sort it out. I did not want Paul Crittenden's death to be murder so I knew I would have to guard against rationalization and selective memory.

First of all, how about those noises last night? Had I, in fact, heard someone moving in the rocks? Had I really heard something like the sound of breaking glass? The pickup horn had been battering at my nerves and eardrums for many minutes and those other sounds would not have been loud. On the other hand, for what reason would my mind play such tricks on me as to make me think I had heard them if they were not real? It's easy to say hallucination under the stress of the moment but would I have hallucinated those particular sounds under those circumstances? I shook myself impatiently. I was asking the wrong questions. Those were questions that I could not answer and were therefore pointless.

Begin again. If I had heard someone moving in the rocks, who might it have been and for what reason would he have been there? Whoever it was hadn't answered when I called out but had presumably continued on his way as silently as possible. Be bold in your thinking, I admonished myself, and call this problematical person the murderer. Very well, what reason would the murderer have had for being there at that time? That was easier. Whatever means he had used to cause Paul to run off the road, it had been something that demanded his presence afterwards to remove or remove the signs of. It was something tangible, then. There was physical evidence of the murder, or at least there had been.

So far, so good. Take the sound of breaking glass next. That would almost certainly be connected to the evidence, if not the evidence itself. It could have been a flashlight or lantern of some kind. I thought of the lanterns that park rangers kept to lend to people who wanted to examine lava caves. They were fairly large metal contraptions with glass enclosing the gas wick. Paul had said the word light twice that I was sure of. Somehow, his murderer had used light to cause him to run off the road. A spotlight would do it. Shine a spotlight in any driver's eyes and he would probably run the car off the road.

Some guys used spotlights for nighttime poaching. A bright light shone directly into a deer's eyes immobilized it, making it easy prey. Jackrabbits, too. They froze right in the path of the car when the headlights caught them. I tried to remember how the tracks were on the road where Paul had gone over. I didn't think there had been any off to the side where a car or pickup would park in order to aim a spotlight to catch Paul's eyes. Well, however it was done, Paul had been killed and I was damned if whoever did it was going to get away with it if I could help it.

I thought about the motive. Paul was old. He'd been born before the Civil War -- that made it seem like an incredibly long time ago. That would make him in his late eighties or early nineties. It was hard to believe that anyone would deny him the few years he had left, especially when he was hale and hearty and still enjoying life. I caught myself up -- that would be why someone wanted to murder him, because he was hale and hearty and had a few years of life left. Because the motive was almost certainly money, the need for money or maybe just the greed for money. I couldn't imagine any other reason for murdering Paul. Any kind of love triangle or jealousy was ludicrous; he wasn't a threat to anyone's safety; and revenge was out of the question, Paul was such a sweet old man.

I yanked myself up short again. I didn't know any of that. The Paul I was acquainted with -- and I had only known him two days -- was an old sweetie but there must have been other sides to his character. I concluded that I didn't really know enough about him or the people around him to postulate most of the motives for murder. I did know that he was a very rich man and I assumed that his children and grandchildren stood to inherit. Assumptions were tricky things, though. I realized that I didn't, really, have any idea how Paul had left his money and property.

By the time I reached the turn-off to Camp Five, I had decided that I needed to talk to Laine if I was going to make any progress. On the other hand, the authorities had evidently written it off as a bona fide accident and it was no business of mine to start yelling murder. I had no information or evidence that the police didn't have. "Except a shard of glass," piped up the imp in my head who makes it her business to keep me from getting too complacent. I decided that my best bet would be to mind my own business.

Delphine Granville was skipping along the road, going toward Schuylers', no doubt to play with Ruby. Both little girls were in the first grade and they spent a lot of time together. As I parked next to my cottage, I saw Lyle Allston and Mason Troupe coming up the Old Road that led to Kinzua. They were in the upper grades room and I knew them well. They had probably been out in the woods, messing around at whatever it is boys do. When you ask them, they usually say they've been doing nothing. All I know is, the doing of nothing takes an astonishing amount of time and energy.

It was good to be back home in my own little niche. I lugged my suitcase in and set it in the bedroom. I would deal with it later, but I felt I couldn't face those filthy jeans right then. The first thing I did was drink a glass of water. The thing I always missed most away from home was the wonderful cold, crisp spring water. I lit the oil heater then kicked off my shoes and curled up on the couch under the afghan. I had a new P.G. Wodehouse novel and if he couldn't keep me amused, it was bleak, indeed. Bertie Wooster had just gotten his affairs in a seemingly hopeless tangle with Jeeves intoning a dolorous, "Most disturbing, sir," when I fell asleep.

It was dark when I wakened and I had a confused idea that there was something urgent that I needed to tend to right away. When I came fully awake, I realized that a trip to the women's bath house was indicated, my little two-room cottage lacking a bathroom. I slipped on my shoes and grabbed a jacket and went over to it. That early in the spring, it was cold but light streamed out of the windows of nearly every house, giving the camp a homey, cozy feeling. I thought about going over to see Uncle Miles and Aunt Genevieve then decided not to. I was tired and not really in the mood to be cheery company.

My dinner was a couple of waffles with pears for dessert. I'd canned the pears myself the summer before and if I do say so myself, they were delicious. After I cleaned up the dishes, I took my tea into the living room portion of the front room and sipped it while I had another go at Bertie and Jeeves. By nine o'clock I was ready for bed.

When I woke at five the next morning, I was rested, invigorated, and ready to face the school day, even the Miller twins. It seemed months since I'd been in the schoolroom, instead of just two days, so much had happened. I finished unpacking my suitcase and slid it to the back of my closet, then did a little housework, dusting and sweeping, that I hadn't had time to do before my trip to Bend. After a leisurely breakfast of oatmeal and coffee, I dressed for school.

The children were all present: the fifth grade, consisting of the Miller twins; the sixth grade, made up of Ray Troupe, Doreen Cranston, and Bobby Cabusap; the seventh grade, comprised of Lyle Allston, Cynthia Masour, and Darla Ziegler; and the two eighth graders, Mason Troupe and Twyla Schuyler. We all took our places with bright, shining faces and resumed the process of education. So far the children had taught me much more than I had taught them but I had hopes of evening the score some day soon.

I got them through the morning's work and was feeling relieved that nothing untoward had disturbed the day. The blow fell at afternoon recess. The Miller twins, Debbie and Dottie, were very bright, inquisitive, and precocious. When they met anything they didn't understand, they did not rest until either they understood it or understood that understanding would have to come later, if at all. While I applauded their wide-ranging quest for knowledge, I dreaded the questions for which I had no answers. I had learned to be very cautious about assigning them subjects for reports because they were never content to rely solely on the encyclopedia for information and I didn't necessarily want to do major research in order to grade their papers.

A year or so ago they had invented a language that they called Quoskeen and spoke it to one another as other children speak pig-latin. Since they were the only ones in the world who understood Quoskeen, their schoolmates were often understandably irritated and exasperated when they spoke it. They were deep in a discussion, conducted entirely in Quoskeen out on the playground; the other children were playing on the swings and monkey bars and playing tag. Sylvia Ziegler, who taught the lower four grades, had dismissed her room and they were trooping off to their various homes. She and I were standing on the front steps chatting when the twins joined us. They waited politely until I finished telling Sylvia about going crazy and buying six yards of velvets and brocades in Bend Friday night. She laughed and said she had a box of fabric lengths that she'd bought one time or another and had never gotten around to making up.   "I ought to get them out and see if I can use some of it for Twyla. She's going to need a whole new wardrobe when she starts high school next fall."

"She can sew, too, can't she?" I asked. "Maybe she'd like to make some of it up."

"Maybe." Sylvia smiled at the twins. "Well, girls, I can see that you have something you want to talk to Miss O'Connor about. I'll see you tomorrow, Marge."

Sylvia went into her schoolroom and Debbie burst into speech.

"We've got a question, Miss O'Connor."

"Yes, Debbie?"

"How can something that's transparent cast a shadow?" Dottie demanded.

I examined the question carefully, looking for the stigmata of riddles, jokes, and conundrums. Seeing none, I requested clarification.

"I don't think I quite understand," I said. "Do you mean like a pane of glass?"

"Water." Debbie said the word as if it were the cornerstone of her belief system. "How can water cast a shadow?"

I felt as if I were going down for the third time. I glanced at my watch and found it was mercifully time to call the children back to their classes.

"I'm afraid we're out of time. If you like, you may stay after school and we'll discuss this further."

Debbie and Dottie exchanged glances and a few

words in Quoskeen, then Dottie told me they would appreciate that. I was not enthusiastic. I blew the whistle and we all went inside to a new set of spelling words for the week. It seemed like a bad omen when the fifth grade spelling book gave us "lucidity" in the week's list.

I dismissed them all at three-thirty and most of them gleefully made a break for the outdoors. Debbie and Dottie came up to my desk to continue our discussion.

"Okay, girls, what exactly is it that you want to know?"

"Okay, it's about water. Sometimes it casts a shadow and sometimes it doesn't," Debbie stated.

"But water is clear, transparent. So how can it cast a shadow?" asked Dottie.

"And why does it cast a shadow only sometimes? It seems as if it would either not cast a shadow at all or cast it all the time," Debbie explained.

I must have looked blank -- I know I felt blank -- because Dottie took pity on me.

"Come into the bathroom," she said, "and we'll show you what we mean."

I sighed, knowing my ignorance was about to be exposed, and allowed the twins to lead me to the lavatory. Debbie filled the basin about two-thirds full of water.

"See?" Dottie asked. "When the water is still, there's no shadow."

Debbie put her hand in the water and agitated it a bit.

"Now look," Debbie said. "See? There are shadows all over the bottom. What causes them? It can't be the water, because the water is transparent."

"And it can't be the motion," Dottie continued, "because motion doesn't cast a shadow."

Both girls looked at me hopefully. Double damn and triple hell, I thought. I don't know what causes the shadow. I didn't say anything, just stared at the shadows on the bottom of the basin.

"And look at this," Debbie said, taking a drop of water on her finger and holding it near the top of the basin. "You can see through the water to my finger but now watch." She turned her finger so the drop depended from it for a moment and I could clearly see the shadow of the water drop on the white of the basin.

"Have you asked your dad about it?" I inquired.

Both girls nodded vigorously.

"He said he didn't know," Dottie said.

"He said we should ask you," Debbie added.

"He did, did he?" I made a mental note to return the favor sometime soon.

"So what causes the shadows?" Dottie repeated.

100

"Well," I began lamely, "it has to do with light reflection and refraction. I don't know exactly how it works or how to explain it. I'll see if I can find out, or at least find out where you can look it up."

"We already tried the Encyclopedia Britannica," Debbie offered.

"It referred us to about ten different volumes but we never did find any explanation," Dottie explained.

"No, I knew it wouldn't be as easy as that."

I pulled the plug in the basin and shooed the girls out of the lavatory and out of the schoolhouse. Lights and shadows, I thought, as I gathered up my papers and prepared to leave. Lights, Paul had said as he lay dying. Lights glared, glistened, glowed, beamed, radiated, shimmered, glimmered, illuminated, flickered, and a whole host of other verbs. Shadows were composed of the penumbra and the umbra, I could remember that much. I seemed to recall a third part but couldn't bring it to mind. Then I wondered what I thought I was doing, standing there thinking about shadows and lights. It made no sense at all. I went home.

Chapter 7

After school I dropped my papers off at home and went to visit Aunt Genevieve. She and Uncle Miles were the handsomest couple I knew. She must have been nearly fifty but she was still lovely, even in a housedress after she'd been cooking and cleaning all day. When I got there she was sitting in her easy chair, knitting something pale blue, looking positively radiant. The house was filled with the deliciously tantalizing aroma of baking spice cake. My mouth began to water as soon as I opened the door.

"Margie, come right in. How are you? How was your trip to Bend?"

Aunt Genevieve stopped knitting and beamed up at me with a big smile. I went over and kissed her cheek.

"Fine, Aunt Genevieve. I'm fine. I'm going to buy a lovely Appaloosa mare named Lotsa Spots."

I dropped down into Uncle Miles' chair and

smiled at my aunt. She glanced at her watch and jumped up, laying her knitting in the seat of her chair. She bustled into the kitchen and I squirmed around in the chair to watch her. She took a couple of pot holders and opened the oven door, peering in dubiously.

"Spice cupcakes for Miles' lunch bucket," she said, poking at one. "I think they're done."

She set two pans of cupcakes on top of the stove and then transferred the cupcakes in their pastel papers to a plate on the drainboard to cool.

"Want one, Marge? There's some cider out on the back porch."

"Sure, I want one. Just the smell makes me hungry. I don't know anything better than your spice cake warm from the oven."

I took a couple of glasses out to the back porch and found the cider jug on a shelf. I filled the glasses and took them into the kitchen. Aunt Genevieve was putting a plate of cupcakes on the table. We sat down and I bit into a little bit of heaven.

"These are scrumptious, Aunt Genevieve. You're the best cook I know. Although I met one last weekend who could run you a darn close second."

"Practice, dear. Practice makes perfect and goodness knows I've had plenty of practice."

"You have, indeed."

"Phil is coming home day after tomorrow."

That explained her radiance. She adored her son and was never happier than when she could cook for him and fuss over him. Fortunately, he adored her, too, so everything was hunkey-dorey when he was home for a visit.

"He hasn't broken anything, has he?" I asked her that because, as a rodeo rider, he had broken an assortment of his bones, some of them twice, and usually brought them home to heal. When he wasn't rodeoing, he worked as a cowboy, sometimes wrangling stock, sometimes wrangling dudes.

"No, not that he mentioned anyway. He's just coming for a visit. His letter said he'd be here a week or maybe two before going to Wickenburg. He's taken a job at the Rocking B."

"That's a dude ranch, isn't it?"

"Mmmmm-hmmmmm."

"I met one of Phil's friends last weekend. Laine Crittenden. His grandfather is the one who sold me the mare. Or was going to sell me the mare, I haven't actually bought her yet. Mr. Crittenden was killed Saturday night."

Aunt Genevieve made an exclamation of surprise and concern. "What a shame. What was it? An accident of some kind? He was quite elderly, I know."

"You know the Crittendens?"

"Well, I don't actually know them, no. But I've heard Phil speak of them. He and Laine were close friends at one time. And, of course, the Appaloosas are very well known in this part of the world."

"He had a wreck with his pickup. He'd gone out to check on a stock tank, to see if the windmill was working all right, and on the way back he ran off the road and the pickup flipped over and he was thrown out. Laine and I went to look for him when he was late getting back. He was still alive when we got there."

"Oh, Margie, how awful for you. And for Mr. Crittenden, too, of course."

I patted her hand reassuringly. "It was pretty awful. I stayed with him while Laine went to call for the ambulance. It was too late, though, when they got there, he was already gone."

"You poor child. It's a dreadful thing to see someone hurt and not be able to help."

"That's exactly how it was. I guess you must have seen a lot of that kind of thing."

For the first time I thought about Aunt Genevieve as a vulnerable human being. She was a nurse and had always been so capable and helpful that I had always assumed, childlike, that nothing was beyond her. Her children, my cousins Phil and Lorraine, and

I had always taken our scrapes and bruises and hurt feelings to her and she had always soothed the hurt away, even if it took the sting of iodine to begin the process.

"Some. I suppose any nurse sees cases in which she can't be of much use but I've been fortunate enough to be able to do something for most of my patients."

"The doctor who came out in the ambulance said no one could have done anything for Paul. They think he must have had a stroke or a heart attack that caused him to run off the road."

I stirred uneasily and reached for another cupcake.

"There's something else, though, isn't there Marge?" Aunt Genevieve asked gently.

I nodded. "I'm not sure it was completely accidental. See, this is how it was."

As I heard myself explaining the circumstances, I wondered if it wasn't accidental after all. There wasn't really anything that definitely ruled it out.

"Well, that's not much to go on," Aunt Genevieve said thoughtfully. "But intuition is often a very good guide to the truth. It doesn't do to ignore it and place all of our faith on tangibles. Were they going to do an autopsy?"

"I don't know. I think so. Laine was just as

puzzled as I am."

"What about the rest of the family? You said both of his aunts were there and some of his cousins?"

"Two cousins. Janet seemed nice enough but Brad is a real jerk. The aunts weren't very friendly."

"To you, you mean?" Aunt Genevieve smiled. "That doesn't mean much, they were under a lot of strain just then."

"I didn't mean friendly to me. They weren't but I really meant friendly to Laine or even each other."

"Well, if Mr. Crittenden had made Laine a partner, they would probably be thinking about how that would affect their own inheritances. That's not considered very nice but it's a very natural reaction. And they both have children and grand-children that they would be concerned for, too."

I nodded. "Sure, I see that. Laine said they all had enough to be comfortable but none were really wealthy."

"Did any of them need money especially?"

"I have no idea about that. Laine said one uncle is an assistant prison warden and the other runs a flight school. His father owns a pear packing house near Medford. He has his own plane so he must be doing pretty well."

Aunt Genevieve made a gesture of impatience. "There's no point in us sitting here speculating."

"You're right." I stood up. "I'm going to the store and then home to grade papers. Do you need anything?"

"No, Miles and I went to Umatilla Saturday and stocked up on everything. Wait a minute, while I whip up some frosting and I'll send some of the cupcakes with you. We can't eat them all before they get stale."

"I'd better not, they're too irresistible. Thanks, Aunt Genevieve."

She walked to the door with me.

"You're welcome," she said.

I walked up the hill to the tiny company store. There was a cocker spaniel sitting alertly by the door so I knew that Richanne Worley was shopping. Duchess never let her get too far away, if she could help it. Richanne came out, carrying a bottle of vanilla extract, as Duchess and I were greeting each other.

"Hi, Richanne, what's for supper tonight?"

Richanne runs the cookhouse for the bachelors and usually she's deep in preparations for six o'clock supper by this time of day.

"Swiss steak and banana cream pie. Gotta get some fruit into them, you know."

"It's getting kind of late to be baking pies. Do you need some help?"

"Oh, no. Thanks just the same." Richanne looked a little puzzled then she smiled. "Oh, the vanilla? It's for the whipped cream. The pies have been done since morning but I ran out of vanilla for the whipped cream."

She went on up toward the cookhouse and I went into the store. Lewis was restocking shelves, putting boxes of wooden matches next to rolls of waxed paper. He looked around when I came in the door and smiled.

"Hi, Marge, how are you this afternoon?"

"I'm fine. How are you?"

"Fair to middlin'. I hear Phil's coming home for a week or two."

The door opened and Nick Garvey came in. Nick was a pal of Phil's when they were growing up. I'd never been too fond of him but he was a nice enough guy. He'd dropped out of high school in his first or second year and had enlisted in the army as soon as he was old enough. He had just come back from Greenland, of all places. His parents had moved to Bly, down in southern Oregon, while he was away so I was kind of surprised when he'd come back to camp and got a job setting chokers. There had been rumors that he'd gotten married overseas but he was living in a bunkhouse with the other bachelors. Lewis and I nodded to acknowledge his presence and continued our conversation.

"Yes, Aunt Genevieve's all excited about it. It'll be nice to see him, he hasn't been home since last fall, right after Pendleton."

"Who's coming home? Ol' Phil? I ain't seen Phil in a coon's age. A couple of coons' ages."

Nick went around behind the mail boxes and checked to see if there was anything for him. There evidently wasn't but it reminded me that I hadn't checked.

"Yes, he's supposed to be here in a day or two," I said, putting a bottle of milk on the counter.

Nick crossed over to the candy bars and I went back of the mail boxes. There was nothing for me but a solicitation to join the Readers Digest Condensed Book Club.

"That sure was nice, him winning the calf roping. I wish Kate and I could have been there to see it," Lewis said.

"I missed it, too. I've gone almost every year since he's been going to Pendleton but I missed his first big win. Maybe he'll do even better this year."

"When was that?" Nick asked. "Last year?"

"Yes, last year at Pendleton. He won the wild cow milking at Calgary the year before." I shook my head mournfully. "He didn't seem too excited about it, though."

Nick guffawed and Lewis laughed.

I had been gathering things up as we talked and Lewis had been keeping an eye on my progress. Seeing that I was finished, he came over to the cash register. I don't know why he bothered with a cash register, I was the only one in camp who paid cash, unless someone had visitors from away -- everyone else charged their groceries and gas and the company deducted it from their paychecks, just as for garbage collection and electricity. We didn't have to worry about phone bills, the only phone in camp was in the office attached to the truck shop and it only connected to the company office in Kinzua.

"That Phil -- what a character he is. I remember one time, him and me and ol' Rudy Ketchum -- you remember Rudy, don't you?"

"I've heard the name but I've never actually met him," I said.

Lewis shook his head.

"Well, he's a case, Rudy is. This one time the three of us was deer huntin' up one of them canyons out of Ukiah. Rudy wasn't feeling too good one morning so Phil and me left him in camp and we went up the canyon, him on one side and me on the other. It was pretty steep and the day turned off to be a hot one, too. Phil, he spooked a big old buck and it come runnin' my way. I got a good clear shot at it and brought it down. Phil come over and helped me gut it and carry it back down the canyon to where our camp was. It was a heavy son-of-a-gun, too. Well, when we finally got back to camp, there was that damn fool Rudy, he couldn't never leave things alone, always had to be foolin' with something. He'd took the headlights out of the pickup and haywired 'em up in a couple of trees and took the battery out and rigged it up so's it would run the lights. He was just so proud and happy, said camp would be bright as noontime all night if we wanted. It didn't work out that way, though. Rudy's schemes never worked out like he thought they was going to."

Nick seemed to think he'd told the whole story and went off into gales of laughter. I waited until he had run down a bit before I asked him what had gone wrong with the lighting idea.

"Oh, Rudy, he dropped the battery on a big ol' rock and busted it open. Battery acid was splashed all over and there we was marooned ten-twelve miles from the nearest gas station. Phil and me pointed out to him that his scheme had blew a fuse and we wasn't one damn bit better off than before and in fact was worse off, because not only didn't we have no lights, we didn't have no pickup that would run, neither. So we sends ol' Rudy down the road talkin' to himself, to hike into Ukiah and get a new battery.

112

Then Phil and me, we set down and had venison steak and played poker by the camp fire until bedtime. Rudy, he never got over that, he claimed the walk to town lamed him permanent. It never, though, he walked fine except when me or Phil was watchin', then he'd limp something awful."

Lewis and I joined in Nick's laughter that time, although I didn't think the whole episode was nearly as funny as he did. I gathered my bag of groceries up and left before Nick could remember any more hilarious anecdotes involving ol' Phil.

"I'll be sure to tell Phil you're back, Nick," I said, as I went out the door. "'Bye, Lewis."

They both called farewells after me and I went on down the hill to my cabin thinking how nice it was to be surrounded by friends, even if they did get on your nerves sometimes. What I had missed most when I was going to college in Ashland was familiar faces. Ashland is a very small town but to me, coming from the much smaller town of Heppner, it had seemed like a city. I smiled at myself -- now, coming from Camp Five, Heppner seems like a city.

The evening was peaceful and pleasant. I roasted a chicken for dinner (and another three or four meals) and served it with a baked potato and green beans. After the cupcakes at Aunt Genevieve's, I didn't need dessert. Shadows on the bottom of the sink as I did the dishes reminded me that I hadn't done anything toward finding out the answer to Debbie and Dottie's question about how a transparent substance can cast a shadow. Drat those twins, anyway. I spent the evening grading papers and bringing my grade and attendance books up to date. Report cards would be due the end of next week.

The next day was typical for the place and time. It was sunny and bright and the general feeling in the schoolroom was one of high good humor. I assigned topics for short essays to the sixth and seventh grades but reading assignments for the fourth and fifth. I just didn't think I could cope right then with whatever the Miller twins' would come up with. They were entirely too original -- I wondered if maybe I could get them started writing poetry. That should be relatively innocuous and even if they wrote in Quoskeen, it wouldn't greatly matter. After all, poetry is supposed to be mysterious, abstruse and recondite -- otherwise poets would write in prose.

There was a breeze most of the day so the mud was drying rapidly. The boys wanted to improve the baseball diamond so they could more closely approximate the way the game is supposed to be played. The school playground consisted of a more or less level area in front with a couple of swings and a set of monkey bars but the ground sloped gently on

114

the west side of the school, toward the meadow. It was covered with native grass that had never been mowed and probably never would be and littered with stones, some baseball size and some football size. I told them they were welcome to lay out a baseball diamond on the slope and hoped it would occupy them for a long time because there were only ten pupils in the upper four grades and only four of them were boys. Doreen Cranston was quite athletic and liked to play baseball and run in sack races and so forth but five is pretty far short of enough kids for two teams.

I didn't need anything at the store but after school I wandered up to see if I had any mail. I was quite surprised to find an envelope with the Happy Appy Ranch return address. I waited until I got home to open it; it was from Laine and the contents were so astonishing I had to read it twice to make sure I understood it.

Laine wrote that an autopsy had been done on Paul and no evidence of either stroke or heart attack had been found. There was nothing to indicate any physical weakness or infirmity that might have caused his accident. He put "accident" in quotation marks. That was surprising enough but more surprising still, he wanted to come up Saturday and talk to me. I didn't want him to come. I wanted his problem, whatever it was, to stay down there on his ranch and not to impinge on my peace and serenity. Then my other self sneered and asked me how I'd slept the night before, pointing out that tossing and turning until nearly dawn did not signify either peace or serenity.

I sighed and sat down to write a note to Laine, telling him to come ahead. My conscience wasn't going to let me rest until I'd done whatever I could to help Laine. I told him that Phil would also be in camp over the weekend and said maybe he could help us figure things out.

Chapter 8

Sylvia Ziegler was quite a lot older than me, in fact, her granddaughter was in my seventh grade class. A family catastrophe had made it expedient for Darla to live with her grandparents and it seemed to work out well. Sylvia had been teaching for nearly twenty years -- she had taken ten or twelve years off when her children were young -- and she was a great help to me. This was my first year of teaching and I was beginning to realize how much I didn't know.

We had decided to give a spring concert with our combined classes. Sylvia had a book of plays and we had worked together on adapting one of them so there were parts for all nineteen pupils. It was a happy little story involving talking daffodils, singing bluebirds, pirouetting fairies, a thunderstorm, and a smiling sun. The girls threw themselves into it with zeal but the boys in the upper grades had balked until we added the thunderstorm and let them throw lightning bolts around and bang on a sheet of metal to simulate thunder. They had wanted to sprinkle rain, too, but we had to veto that as it would spoil the crepe paper costumes. The older kids would also sing and recite.

Sylvia and I were in her room after school, working on the yellow daffodil costumes when my cousin Phil strolled in. I dropped my scissors and the daffodil petals I was cutting out and flew across the room to give him a hug but stopped a couple of paces from him.

"You aren't broken anywhere, are you?" I demanded.

He grabbed me and whirled me around a couple of times, finishing with a bear hug.

"Who, me? Of course I'm not broken -- bent a little here and there, that's all."

He turned loose of me and gave me a big grin, then turned his attention to Sylvia.

"Mrs. Ziegler," he said, beaming at her, "how are you? If you're as well as you look, you're in top notch health, indeed."

"You're just as full of blarney as ever, Philip, but thank you."

I sat down at the worktable and picked up the scissors and yellow crepe paper. Phil pulled up a chair and Sylvia and I laughed when he sat down. Phil is tall and slim and the chair was one of the diminutive ones made for children, Sylvia and I occupying the only two chairs for adults in the room. His knees weren't actually up by his ears but he looked pretty comical.

"Just like old times, Mrs. Ziegler." Phil grinned at us. "Mrs. Ziegler was my teacher in the third and fourth grades," he reminded me.

"I'm sure it's something she's trying to forget," I laughed.

"Not at all," Sylvia chimed in. "Phil was always charming. He did as little studying as possible, but he was never quarrelsome nor disruptive."

She gave Phil a serene smile of approval. Oddly enough, considering that his parents were so good-looking, Phil wasn't a handsome man, being merely pleasant to look upon. I noticed, though, that he was popular with women of all ages.

Phil picked up the daffodil bonnet that I had just finished and set it on top of his head, gazing solemnly at Sylvia and me. We both burst out laughing, he looked so droll with the yellow petals framing his face.

"Is there a song that goes with this bonnet?" he asked.

"There is," Sylvia gasped, "but I couldn't stand for you to sing it."

Phil stood up, grasped the sides of his jeans,

made a mock curtsey, and began to sing "I'm a Little Teapot." Sylvia and I simply shrieked with laughter. When he had tipped himself up and poured himself out, we applauded. He took off the bonnet and sat down with a self-satisfied smile while we wiped the tears out of our eyes. He waited until we had sobered down before he delivered his message.

"Marge, Mother wants you to come to dinner tonight to celebrate the return of the prodigal son."

"I'd be delighted," I said.

"Speaking of dinner," Sylvia exclaimed, "it's time I was getting home to get it started. Max'll be home soon."

Sylvia and I put away the costumes and crepe paper, then Phil and I went into my classroom to get the papers I needed to take home. I heard Sylvia close her classroom door so I locked the porch door as Phil and I left. He went home and so did I.

I didn't want to go to dinner empty handed so I mixed up a corn pudding and put it in the oven. Whatever Aunt Genevieve was serving as the main dish, corn pudding would be a good side dish. While it baked, I graded my papers, pausing a couple of times to marvel at the inventiveness of children. It would surely be much less trouble to read the chapter than to try to bluff through the quiz. I wondered if Mason Troupe really thought the "Portuguese" were a kind of migrating birds. After all, the subject was geography, not biology or nature study.

The corn pudding turned out well -- at least it looked and smelled delicious when I took it out of the oven. Leaving a lamp on in the living room so I wouldn't have to come back to a dark house, I put the pudding in a cardboard box and carried it to Uncle Miles' and Aunt Genevieve's. I helped Aunt Genevieve dish things up and we all sat down to feast on baked ham, scalloped potatoes, and all the fixings. Uncle Miles and Phil kept us in stitches trying to top each other in telling tall tales of their adventures, and they had both had some exciting experiences. After we finished the dishes, Aunt Genevieve and I joined the men in the living room.

"I told Miles about poor old Mr. Crittenden," Aunt Genevieve said to me.

"Crittenden? Paul Crittenden?" Phil asked.

I nodded. "I was there last weekend to see about buying a horse and he was killed in an accident."

Phil expressed his sorrow and I gave him the story.

"I got a letter from Laine yesterday," I told them. "He's going to come to see me Saturday. They did an autopsy on Paul and didn't find anything that would account for him running off the road like that. He wants to talk it over with me."

"Why? Why should he think you know anything you haven't already told him?" demanded Uncle Miles a little truculently.

"I don't think it's exactly that," I answered. "He put the word "accident" in quotes so he evidently isn't convinced it was an accident."

"You mean it was murder?" Phil asked skeptically.

I shrugged. "I don't know. I just don't know. I don't see how it could have been, really. At least I have kind of an idea how it might have been done but it's pretty far-fetched."

"Who would want to murder him, though? He was pretty old, pushing ninety anyway," Phil said.

"I know. You'd think whoever did it could have waited a little longer. He couldn't have had many years left."

Uncle Miles took a Lucky from his pocket and snapped his Zippo to light it.

"How do you think it might have been done, Marge?" he asked, through a cloud of smoke.

"Well..." I was hesitant to air my theory because I wasn't sure what I postulated was actually possible.

"Come on," said Phil impatiently. "If it's hare-brained, we'll let you know and then you can quit worrying about it."

I laughed a little, and Uncle Miles and Aunt

Genevieve laughed too, in a nice kind of way, amused at my little impracticalities. Phil's laughter was more derisive. I had said and done enough idiotic things to have earned a place in the family annals as a comedienne when it came to physics or math.

"Okay, you can all tell me if this is possible or not. When Paul was dying, he managed to say a few words. Not clearly, but I could make some of them out. 'Lights' was one of them; he said that twice and he seemed urgent about it but I couldn't see any relevance. I mean, there weren't any car tracks that we couldn't account for, so it couldn't have been on-coming car lights in his eyes blinding him and making him run off the road."

Uncle Miles scowled. "You're sure about that, Margie?"

"Pretty sure. Laine and I looked and the only tracks that went much past the scene of the accident were Paul's own going out to see to the windmill and coming back. The ambulance and Laine's pickup stopped at about the point where the pickup went over and that jerk cousin of his left tracks only a hundred feet or so past that point."

"But you thought of another way he might have been blinded by lights?" Aunt Genevieve asked.

I nodded. "I ran into Nick Garvey in the store a

day or two ago and he told me a long story about a hunting trip Phil and he and another guy had gone on."

Phil grinned. "Nick's back from the army, is he?"

Uncle Miles stubbed his cigarette out. "Oh, yes, he's back. He's setting chokers for me. Of all the dimwits I've ever been saddled with, he's about the dimmest. He was settin' chokers for Cory Blevens and last week he did something extra dumb, I never did know exactly what, but Cory nearly had a stroke, he got so mad."

Phil laughed. "Good old Nick. He's always good for a chuckle. I'll have to look him up."

"You do that," Aunt Genevieve said. "He's living in one of the bunkhouses. I'd just as soon you'd go see him as to have him here. I don't want him to get to be a nuisance hanging around."

"I thought you liked Nick, Mom."

"I like him well enough but that doesn't mean I want him underfoot. He's like a puppy, you know, always eager for company and never knowing when it's time to go home."

"All right," Phil laughed, "I'll go see him and I won't invite him home with me. Now, Marge, what was the brilliant idea that Nick gave you?"

"Well, it was something about the guy who was with you on this hunting trip taking the headlights off the pickup and rigging them up in the trees to light your camp. Only when he got the battery out to run them, he dropped the battery or something and ruined it."

"Rudy Ketchum," Phil said, laughing again. "I'd almost forgotten that hunting trip. You remember," he said to his folks, "I told you about it."

"Seems like I remember something about it, but just refresh our memories, will you?" asked Uncle Miles with a chuckle.

"Rudy stayed in camp one morning when Nick and I went out. When we got back -- with a nice four-point buck that I got, by the way -- Rudy had rigged up the headlights like Marge said and had taken the battery out of the pickup to hook up to them. Only he dropped the battery on a rock and busted it like a ripe watermelon. So we made him walk into Ukiah to get a new one. We were eleven point four miles out; Rudy got a guy to bring him and the battery back and he checked the odometer on the pickup. My gosh, you'd have thought it was eleven hundred miles, the fuss he made."

We all laughed then sobered down when we remembered why Phil was explaining what had happened on his hunting trip. They all looked at me.

"So, I got to thinking. Someone could have set a pair of headlights in the road with a battery to run

125

them and when Paul Crittenden came along, flashed them on suddenly. He would have been startled and pulled the wheel sharply to avoid hitting what he would have thought was an on-coming car."

I watched them anxiously, not wanting them to pronounce me an impractical boob but not wanting it to be possible at the same time.

Uncle Miles and Phil exchanged the kind of looks that men give one another when their women are wandering into what they consider masculine territory.

"It could be done that way," Uncle Miles confirmed.

"There are lots of easier ways to get rid of an old man," Phil said.

"Such as?" challenged Aunt Genevieve. "Any poison apt to be found around a horse ranch wouldn't be that hard to detect by the symptoms before death and the autopsy after. I suppose a bat on the head and a faked falling accident would be possible, but I gather there were always people around him. Guns and knives would be even harder to fake accidents with. I guess suffocation would be possible but there again, an autopsy would probably show fibers of whatever was used in the air passages."

"Besides," I added, "this method is kind of indirect. Shooting and stabbing and suffocating are

126

pretty straight-forward, direct action crimes. Whoever set that booby trap, if someone did, was a small-souled, sneaking coward." I couldn't keep the tears out of my eyes or my voice. "Paul Crittenden didn't deserve to die like that, painfully in the cold and the mud."

The others agreed.

"It was an awful thing, honey," Uncle Miles said. "I never met him but he had the reputation of being a fine and generous man."

"He was a fine man," Phil agreed. "I met him a couple of times with Laine. If there's anything I can do to help, I'll sure enough do it," Phil said.

I swallowed my tears and smiled at him. "Laine will be here Saturday. We can discuss it with him and maybe figure out what to do, if anything can be done."

Aunt Genevieve reached over and patted my hand.

"That's sensible, Margie. No need to go rushing headlong before we know what we've got to deal with."

I stood up.

"I'd better be on my way," I said. "We've all got to be up early tomorrow morning. Except you, Phil. Don't let him sleep too late, Aunt Genevieve, make him get up and help you make mincemeat or

127

something."

"This isn't the time of year for making mincemeat," Aunt Genevieve said deprecatingly. Then she looked thoughtfully at Phil. "I think the ground is dry enough to clean out the flower beds, though."

Phil groaned. "Thanks a lot, Marge. You'll pay for that."

I laughed and put my jacket on. "Good night. Thanks for the dinner and the good company."

I went out filled with the warmth of an evening spent with loved ones. Even the talk of death and possible murder couldn't completely obliterate the happiness of being with them. While we'd been doing the dishes, Aunt Genevieve had said Lorraine and Darren and Lacey had invited us all for Easter Sunday and invited me to ride with them. I had gladly accepted. It had been several weeks since I'd seen Lorraine. She was a year older but we'd been best friends all our lives and it had left a big gap in my life when I'd gone off to college and she'd married Darren O'Murphy and gone to live on his wheat ranch out of Hardman. Their daughter Lacey was about eighteen months old and Lorraine was expecting again.

There was a three-quarter moon that looked cold and remote but shed a radiance over camp. It was

128

about nine-thirty and most of the houses were dark. I was about half-way home when one of Boyd Atkins' cats scampered out from the bushes in Granvilles' yard, ran across the street and disappeared in the shadows cast by Kate Schuyler's lilac bush. The suddenness of her movement when I wasn't expecting it startled me; what frightened me was the sound of footsteps behind me.

There is something about the footsteps of someone unknown behind one at night that is scary. Maybe it is a holdover from the days when our only protection was rocks and clubs and the world was filled with predators much stronger than people. Or maybe it's the result of watching too many movie heroines being stalked in the dark. Whatever the cause, those footsteps nearly panicked me. I stopped myself from running screaming to the nearest house and scolded myself for my cowardice. Whoever was there would be a friend or at least someone I knew. It was probably Phil with a new slant on our earlier discussion. I turned and called softly.

"Who's there? Phil, is that you?"

The footsteps stopped as soon as I turned. There was no answer to my questions. I tried again.

"Phil, if that's you, you aren't funny."

I thought I could see a dark form against the trunk of the big ponderosa pine in Zieglers' front yard but I couldn't be sure. I turned and began to walk swiftly toward my own house. After a couple of steps, I whirled quickly around. A shadowy form dropped down behind the Cranstons' station wagon so quickly that I could almost believe I had imagined it. The silence was horrible beyond anything I can describe. When I turned and began to run, the footsteps behind me began to run, too. I dodged into the women's bath house and looked around frantically for something to either jam against the door or defend myself with. There was a metal wastebasket between the two washbasins and nothing else. There was no way to lock the door, of course.

Cursing the company policy that would not allow me to build a bathroom onto my cabin, I retreated into one of the toilet stalls and pushed the flimsy bolt into its socket. My breath was coming fast and noisily; I tried to regulate it so I could hear whoever was out there.

The door opened and footsteps crossed to the other toilet stall.

"Damn it, no paper!"

I could have cried with relief -- it was Omega Price. Dear Omega.

"Here," I said shakily, passing some under the stall partition, "there's plenty on this roll."

"Marge? Thanks."

Omega took the paper and a moment later she flushed and came out of the stall. I came out of mine, too. She went over to one of the basins and washed her hands, looking at me in the mirror.

"Is there anything wrong? You look funny."

"I don't know. I think I was being followed and I got scared and ran in here."

"Followed? In Camp Five? Who would follow you? And why?"

Omega's skepticism was rapidly returning me to an approximation of normalcy. Who, indeed? Likewise, why?

"I don't know but there was someone behind me and when I asked who it was, there was no answer. Then when I started to run, so did he."

"Did you get a look at him?"

I shook my head.

"No, not really."

"I think you've been reading too many murder mysteries," she said. "Go ahead and do whatever you need to and I'll walk out with you."

I went back into the stall, grateful for her company and at the same time resentful of her assumption of superiority.

"If it was that cougar that was hanging around camp, I could understand. Anybody's got a right to be afraid of a cougar. But a man following you --

131

well, who would it be? All the men are in bed and asleep, or going there now. They have to be up too early to be following you around in the night. Besides, what for? It just doesn't make sense, Marge."

Omega walked me to my house and I stood on the step and waited until she got home to go inside. I knew she was right, that it didn't make sense. Nevertheless, someone had followed me. I went inside and locked the door behind me, thankful that I'd left a light in the living room on. I quickly checked every possible hiding place in my two rooms, paying special attention to the bedroom closet and under the bed. Then I undressed and got under the covers, leaving the living room lamp burning. I knew I wouldn't sleep at all if I darkened the house. As it was, I didn't sleep much.

Chapter 9

I got up at four the next morning and turned off the living room lamp. The men would be starting for the woods in another hour so I felt safe. Whoever it had been the night before was surely not still out there. Nevertheless, I waited until daylight before I left the house. I cooked myself a couple of scrambled eggs with bacon and toast, and made some coffee. I felt fine, then, in daylight, with a good breakfast in me and an interesting weekend to look forward to.

Nothing much happened at school. Doreen and the boys spent recess improving their baseball diamond, throwing the stones off the baselines and finding suitable large flat stones to serve as bases. Most of the girls played some elaborate form of blind man's bluff that Debbie and Dottie had invented. It involved assigning each player a double digit number and the one who was "It" could only tag those players whose number added up to a number greater than "Its" number. For instance, Debbie, who was

#29, could only catch those whose numbers added up to more than 11. Thus, her sister Dottie, who was #36, was immune but Cynthia Mansour (#77) and Twyla Schuyler (#48) were fair game. To keep everyone engaged, even when they were immune to capture, "It" was blindfolded and the others milled around announcing their numbers. There was lots of shrieking and yelling so everyone had a good time.

At lunchtime I walked over to see Phil and tell him about being followed home last night. Aunt Genevieve was just setting out a bowl of creamed tunafish. Naturally, I accepted her invitation to join them and got myself a plate while she took biscuits out of the oven. It was a real treat considering that I usually had a bologna sandwich or something similar for lunch. Aunt Genevieve was inclined to be alarmed about my unseen follower but Phil seemed to think I'd been imagining things.

"It's very vague, isn't it, Marge?" he asked. "I mean, the sound of footsteps in the night doesn't have to be sinister, even at the advanced hour of nine-thirty. It was probably one of the men from the bunkhouses going home from visiting someone. Or maybe one of the older kids going home after spending the evening doing homework with a friend."

I nodded doubtfully. "I know it sounds silly but it

didn't feel silly last night."

"Why didn't the person answer when Marge called out to him?" Aunt Genevieve demanded. "Anyone with a legitimate reason for being out and about would have realized she was frightened and reassured her."

"Not necessarily." Phil gave his mother a somber glance and winked at me. "Maybe whoever it was had been somewhere he shouldn't have been, doing something he shouldn't have been doing."

"Well, yes, we always have to allow for that, even here in Camp Five," agreed Aunt Genevieve.

I was indignant. "You mean an assignation between one of the bachelors and a married woman? Nonsense. It happens but when it does everyone knows about it. There hasn't been anything like that for ages."

"Maybe juvenile delinquency has broken out here. It has everywhere else."

I laughed. "Not a chance. In a community of only about a hundred people, where everyone knows everyone else, the kids don't have a chance to become delinquents. At least not here in camp. I'm not sure what they might get up to when they're away. I don't think we've had so much as a broken window in camp since you and Nick Garvey upset the Browns' garbage can and soaped the store window that Halloween years ago."

We all laughed at the only outbreak of juvenile delinquency any of us could remember in Camp Five. It had seemed serious at the time and the miscreants had been summarily dealt with but time, as Paul Crittenden had remarked, takes the misery out and leaves only the love and laughter.

I went back to school in a much mellowed mood. I still thought I had been followed last night by someone with some sort of malevolence on his mind but I also thought I had probably exaggerated the whole incident. The afternoon went smoothly but by three-thirty I was feeling the effects of my sleepless night. I know I gave the sixth grade spelling test to the fifth grade and vice versa. It didn't matter with the fifth grade because Dottie and Debbie always took all four tests and it didn't make much difference with the sixth grade because none of the three ever bothered much about studying their spelling words anyway. At that, I found when I corrected them in the evening, the sixth grade had done somewhat better than usual. I wondered if any of them except the twins had noticed the difference.

I went to bed early and, reassured by my talk with Aunt Genevieve and Phil, went right to sleep. It was a few minutes past one when I woke up, fear shooting through me. I didn't know what had frightened me -- a noise, a light, a movement. I got up and slid my feet into my slippers, then pulled my robe around me. I kept still, listening and watching, trying to hear or see what had wakened me. Cautiously, I moved into the living room and softly went to the front window. I was peering out when there was a crash of shattering glass in my bedroom. I spun around and the glare of fire arced from the broken window to my bed. Pure instinctive reaction took me to the kitchen sink where I filled a large saucepan with water. I ran to the bedroom and threw it on the bed, then ran back for more water. Even as I was putting the fire out, I was enraged that someone had ruined Grandma Straversky's quilt she had made as a bride.

No heroic measures were needed to douse the fire; it never had a chance to spread or even to burn more than the topmost quilt. As I examined my bed, making sure the fire was completely out, I found a stone. It was ovoid in form, about three by four inches and a couple of inches thick. It must have been used to break the window for a clear shot for the fire bomb.

There was a shout from outside and the sound of the Price's door slamming. Then Cleve Price's voice yelling orders to stop. I heard him running up the slope, toward the bunkhouses where the bachelors lived then I grabbed my keys and, locking the door behind me, ran to Uncle Miles. It didn't occur to me until much later that I might have run into an ambush; at the time all I could think of was Uncle Miles and the safety he represented.

I banged on the door, shouting for Uncle Miles and Phil. A light came on in the hallway and then the living room. Phil and Aunt Genevieve were right behind him when Uncle Miles opened the door.

"Margie! What is it, honey?"

I fell into his arms, sobbing and shaking. At first all I could say was, "Uncle Miles, oh, Uncle Miles."

He comforted me and led me over to the couch. Aunt Genevieve sat down with me and put her arms around me, patting me on the back much as if I were six months old. I don't think I was hysterical for very long but even while I was, I was embarrassed to be acting like a child. I pulled myself together. Uncle Miles hunkered down in front of me, holding my hand, and Phil sat on the arm of the couch, patting my shoulder. As soon as I could, I sat up and tried to smile at them all.

"That's better," Aunt Genevieve said.

She got up and came back with a box of tissues for me. Uncle Miles sat down on the couch beside me, still holding my hand.

"I'm going to put the kettle on," Aunt Genevieve

said. "You've had a shock of some kind, that's plain."

She went out and I could hear her running water and rattling china.

"Now," said Uncle Miles, "tell us what the devil is wrong."

I squeezed his hand, then loosened my grasp so I could mop up.

"I'm sorry," I said, "I'm acting like an idiot. Someone set my bed on fire."

There were exclamations of astonished horror. Phil tore into the kitchen and came back with a shot glass of whiskey. I didn't want it and said so but Aunt Genevieve told me to drink it. It made me shudder but it did give me a nice warm glow. Then I told them all about it and how Mr. Price had chased the man.

Phil and Uncle Miles went to put some clothes on. I gave them my keys and they each took a flashlight and went to my house.

"You'll stay here the rest of the night," Aunt Genevieve told me.

"Thanks, I was going to ask you if I could."

"Come and help me make up the bed in Lorraine's old room."

She got sheets and pillowcases and it was very soothing and comforting to do something so completely normal and ordinary as make the bed. I was back to relative normalcy by the time we finished. We went out to the kitchen and Aunt Genevieve stirred up a pot of cocoa.

"We don't need any more stimulation tonight," she said. "This will help us all get to sleep."

"I don't feel as if I could ever sleep again," I said with a shaky little laugh.

"I can't help thinking this was some kind of mistake," Aunt Genevieve said, sitting down opposite me at the kitchen table.

"I don't know what it was, except some kind of incendiary device aimed at me."

"But who would want to hurt you, Marge? It doesn't make sense. Unless you have some idea?"

I shook my head. "My conscience is reasonably clear. All I can think of is that it's related to Paul Crittenden's death somehow."

"But how? If the police have accepted it as an accident, surely it wouldn't be wise of the murderer, if there was one, to attack you."

"So you'd think."

Uncle Miles and Phil came in just then and peeled off their jackets. Phil took them to the back porch and came back to sit at the kitchen table where Uncle Miles was already lighting one of his Lucky Strikes. Aunt Genevieve brought him an ashtray and poured the cocoa into cups. I jumped up to help and carried two of the cups with their saucers to the table while Aunt Genevieve brought the other two.

"Would anyone like a snack?" she asked. "A cupcake or a sandwich?"

No one would so she sat down and we all looked at one another, suddenly reluctant to talk about the terror of the night.

Finally, Phil said grimly, "It was a Molotov cocktail."

"I'm not very clear on exactly what that is," Aunt Genevieve said. "I've read about them in the paper, of course. They're something that the Russians throw at one another, aren't they?"

"That's right. I'm no expert," said Phil, uncharacteristically modest, "but they're simple to make. Fill a bottle or jar with gasoline, stuff a rag in the top, light and throw. It breaks on impact and the rag sets the gas on fire. Very effective, especially when thrown into a passing car."

Aunt Genevieve closed her eyes and I shuddered.

"Lord have mercy," said Aunt Genevieve softly.

"Cleve was just coming back when we got there," Uncle Miles said, blowing a cloud of smoke up at the ceiling. "He chased the man up towards the truck shop and then lost him. He evidently hid somewhere, behind a tree or one of the bunkhouses."

"If it hadn't been so dark," Phil added, "he said he

could have caught him. The guy wasn't a fast runner."

"Margie," Uncle Miles asked, "what's it all about?"

"I don't know, Uncle Miles. Aunt Genevieve and I were just talking about it. It must have something to do with Paul Crittenden's death but I don't know why I've become a target."

"You must know something, or someone thinks you know something."

"But I don't," I wailed. "I think Paul was murdered, sure, but I haven't the foggiest idea of who murdered him."

"Let's go at this logically," Phil said. "Who wanted Mr. Crittenden to die? Or who might have wanted him to die?"

I shook my head. "I just don't know. There are possibilities but I haven't a shred of evidence that points to anyone."

"What are the motives for killing him?" Phil asked, reasonably.

"Money, I guess."

"There aren't really many motives for murder," Aunt Genevieve said.

Uncle Miles looked at her with surprise. He read westerns but she read murder mysteries. I guess it must have been a little startling for him to hear his

142

wife calmly discussing motives for murder.

"Such as?" he asked, frowning at her through his cigarette smoke.

"Money, fear, jealousy, revenge. And," she added thoughtfully, "there's just plain meanness. Although, I suppose that would technically come under the heading of insanity."

"Okay, who has any of those motives, Marge?" Phil asked.

I threw up my hands helplessly. "I just don't know. I don't know that much about the Crittenden family and friends and neighbors. He was a very wealthy man and some of his family may have needed or wanted their inheritance very badly. But I don't even know how he left his money in his will. Or even if he had a will."

"What family is there?" asked Aunt Marge.

"He had three children, two daughters and a son. They're all married and have grown up children who are also married. There are some step-grandchildren, too."

"Where do they live? Were they there when Mr. Crittenden died?" asked Uncle Miles.

"Laine was but I don't suspect him, he and his grandfather were close. In fact, Paul had made Laine a partner in the business."

"How about the others?" Uncle Miles persisted.

"Laine's dad lives near Medford; he has a packing house there. One of the daughters lives in Reno and the other one lives in Kansas."

"Laine's dad has a private plane, though," Phil put in. "It would take less than an hour for him to fly from Medford to Redmond."

"Well, that would be silly," said Aunt Genevieve. "Someone at the airport would remember that he'd been there. He couldn't keep that a secret."

"I don't know, Mom. He wouldn't have to land at the airport. He could land a lot of different places -- fields, meadows, even roads out a ways where there's not much traffic."

"What about the daughters?" asked Uncle Miles, grinding out his cigarette. "Do you know where they were, Marge?"

"One of them was there visiting -- she and her husband and son and the son's girlfriend got there the night before the accident. The other one came the day after; the one from Kansas, with her husband and one of her daughters and the daughter's husband."

"So presumably they're out of it, anyway," said Aunt Genevieve.

"Not really," I said. "At first I thought they'd probably flown in when Laine notified them but the plates on the car they were driving were Kansas plates."

Phil threw up his hands. "So nobody's out of it, except Laine. The field is wide open."

I gave Phil an apologetic look. "I don't think anyone is completely out of it. I don't think Laine had anything to do with it but as far as I know, he could have. I was riding in the arena at the time Paul went off the road. There was at least an hour between times that I saw Laine, from when he left the arena while Paul gave me a lesson to when he came back, looking for his grandfather."

Uncle Miles rubbed his face with both hands.

"Let's go to bed, get such sleep as we can in what's left of the night." He looked at me sternly, "Margie, you stay here tonight. You're not going to sleep at that house until we find out who's behind this and put a stop to it."

"Okay, Uncle Miles." I gave him a meek smile. "My bed isn't sleepable anyway."

"Besides," Aunt Genevieve said with a grin, "we've already made up the bed in Lorraine's old room. For once, Margie isn't disposed to argue."

I stacked the cups and saucers in the sink while Aunt Genevieve poured hot water from the tea kettle in the empty cocoa pan. When we had all gone to our rooms, Uncle Miles checked the door to be sure it was locked, and turned the lights out. I was standing in the bedroom doorway when he went past and I put out a hand to stop him and kissed him goodnight with a murmured, "thanks." He gave me a smile and told me to hop into bed and not to worry.

I hopped into bed but I didn't even try not to worry. When someone unknown has thrown a Molotov cocktail with the intention of burning you to death, worry is about all you do, if you survive. I was sure that it was somehow tied in with Paul Crittenden's death and that's about all I was sure of. Evidently someone thought I knew something that was or could be dangerous to him. Only, if that was the reason, why wait almost a week before acting?

Who, of those I considered suspects, knew where to find me? Laine Crittenden and Audrey Wells. I couldn't remember if anything had been said in Ricki Fenton's hearing that would tell her where I live, but I didn't consider her a suspect. I didn't see what she would have to gain by Paul's death. Of course, I still didn't know how Paul had left his money and property -- there were enough possibilities there to keep me busy for weeks thinking of them all. Any of Paul's children or grandchildren or their spouses or step-children could be guilty, or any combination of them with or without Ricki's connivance.

I thought about what I'd said about the murderer being a sneak and a coward. Throwing gasoline with a lighted rag at a person's bed certainly fit that pattern. I tried to read the characters of the suspects to see if anyone stood out as definitely either meeting the description or incapable of such actions but I simply didn't know any of them well enough. I didn't think Laine was either a sneak or a coward but I realized that I had only known him a couple of days and, although I liked him a lot and he seemed a fine upright young man, he might very well have character flaws that were not on display.

Lorraine's room was pretty much as she had left it when she married Darren and went to live on his wheat ranch. There were sheer priscilla curtains at the high, single pane windows and a pretty white crocheted spread on the double bed. Her collection of storybook dolls still graced the narrow shelves Uncle Miles had put up for them and her seashells, gathered on many visits to the ocean, still reposed in Mason jars on her dresser. I had a similar collection of seashells at home in Heppner, most of them gathered on the same trips as Lorraine's. I tried to switch my mind from murder to Lorraine and her growing family. During wheat harvest, Lorraine cooked lunch and supper for a crew of about twenty men. She and Darren could afford to pay a cook for a few weeks but both came of thrifty folk who were used to doing for themselves. Lorraine and I were best friends as well as cousins. I was looking forward to seeing her and her little family Easter Sunday.

I tried to concentrate on Lorraine but flames shooting up in the middle of my bed kept intruding. I was tempted to ask Aunt Genevieve for a sleeping pill but decided not to wake her. Plus, it apparently behooved me to stay alert and to keep my wits about me. There were a number of Lorraine's books in a small bookcase under one of the windows so I turned on the bedside lamp and hunted out *A Girl of the Limberlost*. Maybe my mind would accept Elnora's problems as a substitute for the flaming bed.

It worked fairly well; I didn't get any sleep but I did get my mind to stay with the book most of the time. It was daylight when I finished it and I was debating whether to get another book or get up when I heard Aunt Genevieve's bedroom door close. Pretty soon the aroma of perking coffee came floating in to me and pulled me out of bed.

Chapter 10

After breakfast, Phil and I went over to my house so I could get dressed. I was beginning to feel as if I'd worn those pajamas and that robe since the dawn of time. While I put on a pair of pedal pushers and a sweater, Phil went out to look over the ground outside my bedroom window. He and Uncle Miles had looked last night but he wanted to see it in daylight to see if there were any identifiable footprints. I cleaned up the broken glass from the window and gathered up my laundry, including my bedding, to do at Aunt Genevieve's. I would probably be there all day and Saturday was when I normally used her washing machine.

There was a big, irregular burned spot right in the middle of Grandma Straversky's quilt. I hated it that the quilt had been ruined. It was a beautiful thing of exquisite needlecraft. Well, I'd wash it and maybe the undamaged parts could be used for crib coverings for my sister's and Lorraine's babies.

Naturally, I would keep one for my own babies, whenever the need should arise. I set my basket down by the door and pulled on a jacket.

Outside, Phil was standing at the corner of the house talking to half a dozen neighbors. He had evidently already told them about my fire in the night because they were exclaiming their outrage and concern.

"A Molotov cocktail?" Ford Troupe was the powder monkey. Whenever a stump had to be dynamited or obstacles blasted from a road under construction, Ford was the man who set the charge. Just then he was comical in his amazement. "In Camp Five? I don't believe it."

"Dad took it home with him last night," Phil said. "You're welcome to come over and look at it."

"I think I will," Mr. Troupe said, almost truculently.

"What *is* a Molotov cocktail?" Diane Miller was frowning in her effort to understand what had gone on. "I know it's something the Russians throw at one another but I've never known exactly what it is."

Lyle Allston, one of my seventh graders, knew all about it. "It's a kind of bomb, Mrs. Miller. You take a jar or a bottle and fill it with gasoline and put a rag in the top. Just before you throw it, you light the rag. Isn't that right, Mr. Troupe?"

150

He nodded. "That's right. When the jar breaks, the gasoline -- liquid and fumes -- spreads out and the burning rag lights the whole shootin' match. It's an effective little bomb but it's about as dangerous to the one who throws it as to the one who catches it."

"How's that?" Pete Worley asked.

"Well, think about it, Pete," Mr. Troupe said. "You have a jar of gas in your hand and you set fire to it and throw it. If you're not mighty damn careful, you're apt to splash it on yourself when you rare back to throw it."

He mimed throwing and it was easy to see what he meant as he pulled his arm back and then let fly with an imaginary missile. We all nodded our understanding and contemplated the foolhardiness of such an act.

Cleve and Omega Price came out of their house and joined us.

"Mr. Price saw the man who threw it and chased him," Phil said, nodding at the Prices.

"Well, who was it?" Mr. Worley demanded.

"I don't know who it was," Mr. Price said.

"I was so scared," Mrs. Price declared. "I was sound asleep when Cleve all of a sudden jumped out of bed and run out of the house. He yelled at me to stay there and I had no more idea of what was going on or what the danger was than nothing."

Mr. Price fixed an accusing eye on her, "You didn't stay there, neither. When I come back she was standing in the front yard." He shook his head mournfully at the foolhardiness of women.

"Well, but, how did you know there was anyone *to* chase?" Cory Blevins asked.

"I'd got up for a glass of water and when I got back in bed, I glanced at the window and saw something that looked like fire go sailing through the air. I couldn't see the fire, just some kind of fiery glow. Naturally, I went to see about it."

We all nodded understandingly, fire being about the most dreaded catastrophe loggers can think of. Not to mention that the nearest fire truck was eleven miles away.

"Did you get a look at the fellow?" Mr. Troupe wanted to know.

Mr. Price shook his head. "Not a good look. Time I got out the door, he was just a kind of dark spot running up the hill. He wasn't going that fast, I could have caught him if it wasn't for all the cover. He must have hid is all I can think. When I couldn't see him or hear him, I had to give up and come on back home."

"But *why* would anyone throw a bomb at Marge?" Mrs. Miller came over and put her hand on my arm. "Marge? I just can't seem to take it in.

Things like this don't happen in Camp Five."

"That's what I thought, too," I said. "I don't know why anyone would do such a thing. Last weekend I was in Bend and a man died at the place I was visiting. At first we thought it was just an accident but there were some circumstances that didn't fit. All I can think is that Mr. Crittenden was murdered and whoever did it thinks I know something about it. I don't."

"But that was in Bend," Pete Worley said, as if trying to reason with a very small child. "That wouldn't have any connection with Camp Five."

"Crittenden?" Cory Blevens' face took on a look of astonishment. "One of the Crittendens that have that horse ranch? What do they call it? Happy Valley."

"Happy Appy," Phil said. "They raise Appaloosas. Yes, it was old Mr. Crittenden."

"Now that's a shame," Mr. Worley said. "He was pretty old, I guess, but he was still hale and hearty. At least, last time I saw him, he was."

"He still was," I said. "Paul Crittenden. He must have been in his late eighties or early nineties. I only met him last Friday but he was a lovely old man."

"But what happened to him?" Mr. Troupe demanded. "Why should him dying cause someone to throw Molotov cocktails at you?"

"I don't know. Paul had an accident with his pickup Saturday night. He was alone and when his grandson, Laine Crittenden, and I found him, he was lying where he'd been thrown out when the pickup rolled down the hill. He was still alive but he died while I was there. I stayed with him while Laine went to the phone to call the ambulance."

"Look here, Marge, that makes no sense," Mr. Troupe declared. "Not unless it wasn't really an accident. If someone murdered him, then it would make sense. The murderer might think you had tumbled to it that the accident wasn't an accident and be trying to shut your mouth permanently."

"It still makes no sense," Mr. Worley said. "Why wait almost a week? She's had time to tell the whole world if there was anything to tell."

"What did the cops say?" Cory asked. "They must have checked it out. They'd have to with a fatality."

I nodded. "Two sheriff's deputies came out last Sunday morning and took some measurements and took my statement and Laine's. They said it was an accident. I know it doesn't seem to tie in with what happened here last night but it's hard for me to believe that I've suddenly made a deadly enemy."

Several of my neighbors nodded, looking perplexed.

"It's beyond me," Mrs. Miller said. "I just hope the twins aren't going to get interested," she added, sighing deeply.

She went on up the hill toward the store and the rest of us exchanged grins, knowing what havoc Dottie and Debbie could wreak when they got interested in anything.

"Have you called the cops?" Mr. Worley asked.

"As a matter of fact," I said, surprised, "I hadn't even thought of that. I don't know what they could do about it. Uncle Miles and Phil came over last night and couldn't find any indication of who did it. Phil, you looked again this morning, did you see anything helpful?"

"Not a thing. Still, we should call them. Dad put the jar in a saucepan to carry it so if there were any fingerprints, he wouldn't smudge them. Maybe the rag or the jar would help. I'll go up to the office after while and call Mr. Hamilton and get him to call the state police or the sheriff's office. I don't know who has jurisdiction."

The men found that satisfactory and they went their several ways after telling me to be careful and expressing their outrage that I could be attacked in my own home. It was a good feeling to know that all these people were concerned about me and ready to rush to my defense.

Cory Blevens started to walk away but came back after a few steps.

"I'm going home tomorrow," he said. "Dad likes for Guy and me to come to church on Sunday. I'll let Guy know what's been happening here."

I couldn't think of a thing to say except to thank him, rather lamely, I'm afraid. Guy was Cory's younger brother and I had dated him a few times last fall and winter but lately he'd been getting on my nerves. He was a nice enough guy, no pun intended, but my heart had never skipped a single beat on his account. He clerked in Prewitt's Haberdashery in Condon and I just wasn't all that interested in neckties and socks and suits, which were his principal topics of conversation.

Cory and Guy certainly gave the lie to the adage that ministers' children are the wildest kids in town. They were both solid citizens who took their responsibilities seriously and while I appreciate that, I found them both pretty darn stodgy. I reflected on the observation that solid and stolid so often go together in personalities. It was going to be difficult to let Guy know that I didn't want to go out with him anymore without hurting his feelings.

Phil and I were standing on my step when we saw a pickup turn off the main road and come down the hill into camp. I didn't recognize it at first as it came slowly down into camp and took the upper road. The houses hid it from sight for a bit, then it came into view and I saw it was Laine and with him, Audrey Wells. I began to wave madly and he saw me and pulled up beside my Pontiac.

I hurried over to him and almost before he got his feet on the ground I gave him a quick hug and he gave me a light kiss on the cheek. Phil was there by that time and they greeted one another with the roughness that men use to camouflage their softer emotions with each other. Audrey hopped out and she and I hugged briefly and there was a flurry of introductions. Phil took the opportunity to hug Audrey, although he was meeting her for the first time. I gave him my best school marm frown and he winked at me over Audrey's head.

"Phil, you ol' son-of-a-gun," Laine exclaimed, clapping him on the shoulder.

"When you call me that, smile," Phil snarled in mock bluster.

They grinned at one another like chessy cats and shook hands exuberantly. I hadn't realized until then that they were close friends. I guess when you pick up the pieces of a friend left by bucking horses and brahma bulls you do get close.

They turned to Audrey and me and each adjured us to be careful in our dealings with the other as he was a rounder and a reprobate.

"But you know that," Laine said to me, "having known this ol' boy all your life. How you stood it, I don't know."

"How she stood it?" Phil exclaimed. "You sure don't know her very well. She's about the bossiest, most curious, interfering female relative a man was ever saddled with. I could tell you stories -- "

I shot him a mock glance of baleful warning. "Oh, well, if we're going to tell stories, I've got a few I could tell."

Both men laughed. Then Laine looked all around at the houses and the mountains and the meadow, nodding as if he approved of the design. There are few places on earth prettier than the setting of Camp Five but I'm aware that not everyone appreciates it. For some the isolation, in itself, detracts so much from the attractiveness of the place that they fail to see the beauty at all.

"Is this your first visit to Camp Five?" I asked.

Audrey nodded. "I've been all around it but I never had any reason to come here before, or Kinzua, either."

"Me, too," said Laine. "I've been to Kinzua a couple of times but we went in the other way, through Madras and Fossil. This is wonderful."

"It is." Phil said. "Sometimes, when I'm in Texas

or southern California or somewhere like that, I get so homesick for it, I could cry. I've never seen anyplace I'd rather live."

"That must be why you live all over the map," Laine agreed solemnly.

Phil smiled.

"You've always been fiddle-footed," I said. You've always wanted to see what was on the other side of the mountain."

"Yeah, I have. But I've always known that when I do settle down, I'll settle down here." The look on Phil's face changed. "Laine, I'm sure sorry about your grandpa. Marge told us about how he died."

The light died out of Laine's face. "Did she tell you he didn't just die, that he was murdered?"

Audrey moved closer to Laine and his hand reached out for hers.

"Are you sure?" I asked, even though I knew it was a silly question. "What did the autopsy show?"

"Nothing," Laine said. "Nothing that would account for the pickup running off the road like that. No heart attack, no stroke, no injuries other than the ones he got when he was thrown out of the pickup. He was all busted up inside and had some bones broke, but the doc said he was sure the damage was all caused at the 'accident.'"

Nobody spoke for a minute or so while we

absorbed the meaning of the post mortem findings. Finally, I broke the silence.

"We've got a lot to talk about. Come on in and we'll fill you in on what happened here last night."

"Then we'll all pool our ideas. Okay?" Phil asked.

"Sounds okay to me," I said. "Laine?"

"Yeah, sure. Something went on here last night? What do you mean?"

We went into my house and I waved them to chairs while I went to the refrigerator and got a couple of bottles of beer out. I uncapped them and handed one to each of the men with a glass. I didn't pour the beer into the glasses because I knew they would rather drink out of the bottles. I held up a bottle of beer in one hand and a sodapop in the other and looked a question at Audrey. She pointed to the sodapop and, as I don't happen to care for the taste of beer, I got another bottle for myself.

Audrey and Laine were on the couch with Phil in the easy chair opposite them. I brought a kitchen chair to sit in.

"Okay, what happened here last night?" Laine prompted.

"Someone threw a Molotov cocktail at Marge," Phil said.

We both burst out laughing as Laine's and Audrey's mouths dropped open and Laine's eyes

160

bugged out. Then Laine grinned, looking a little sheepish.

"You're kidding, of course. What really happened?"

"No, Phil's telling the truth," I said. "We laughed because it sounds so improbable and you looked so funny. Someone broke my bedroom window last night and lobbed a Molotov cocktail in. That burned smell isn't from my cooking, it's from my Grandmother Straversky's quilt burning."

"But you're okay. You are okay?"

Laine seemed to be having a little trouble assimilating the facts and I didn't blame him. Here, in the middle of the morning, it seemed completely unreal to me, too.

"Yes, I'm okay," I said. "I wasn't in bed when the bomb landed. Something woke me up. I don't know if it was a noise or intuition," (both men snorted at that) "or what. But about ten seconds after I got up, the window smashed and flames shot up from the middle of my bed."

I began to shake again, thinking about it, and Phil came over and moved me to the easy chair. He sat on the arm of the chair and put his left arm around me.

"Okay, Margie," he murmured, "it's okay now."

I smiled at him. "Thanks, Phil. I'm all right."

Phil looked at me doubtfully and kept his arm

where it was. Laine was scowling, trying to understand and Audrey looked horrified and incredulous.

"But, why? Who would want to hurt you, Marge?" she cried.

I shook my head. "I don't know. All I can think of is that it must be tied into what happened to Mr. Crittenden last Saturday."

"Yes," Phil added. "He must have been murdered and whoever did it must think Marge knows how it was done or who did it. It's the only way this attack on her makes any sense at all."

"Well, I agree as far as that goes," Laine said. "But it doesn't go very far. The autopsy showed absolutely no abnormalities whatsoever. I talked to the doctor who did it, Doc Raynor. He said there were the signs of age that you'd expect in a man ninety years old but no signs of disease or recent injury. I think the poor old guy was murdered, too, but I don't see how he could have been."

"I have an idea about that," I said, leaning forward and glancing at Phil. "Phil has an old buddy who's recently come back from his stint in the army, Nick Garvey. I ran into him at the store the other day and he started telling me long, pointless stories about what he and Phil and their friends used to do in the old days. I didn't pay too much attention at the time

162

but later I started thinking about one story he told." I looked at Phil. "I mentioned it to you, the one about the guy who took the headlights and battery out of the pickup while you and Nick were hunting."

Phil nodded. "Sure, Rudy Ketchum."

"Tell Laine about it, Phil. How he rigged up the lights."

Phil explained how headlights could be set up and turned on with a battery and I gave him my theory that it was that kind of a setup that caused Paul to run off the road. Laine nodded thoughtfully.

"I can see how it could work," he said. "But why go to all that trouble? Why not just park a car or a pickup in the road and flash the lights on when Paul got close?"

"He was old and his reflexes weren't that good anymore," I said. "If he had actually hit the other vehicle instead of going off the embankment, how could the murderer explain the damage to his vehicle? Plus, even if it came off, there would be tire tracks to explain away."

"Then, too," Audrey chimed in, "your grandpa was like most old people, he didn't drive that fast, especially after dark. A collision at a slow speed might not be damaging enough to make his death plausible, but the way Marge described how his pickup went off the road and rolled over, he was almost sure to be hurt bad enough to kill him."

Laine nodded. "I see that. God, it's horrible. Someone plotting and planning all that to kill a sweet old man who couldn't have had much time left anyway."

"Laine," I asked gently, "did you bring that glass shard we found in the rocks?"

He pulled a small pillbox out of his pocket, opened it, and handed it to me. Inside was a sliver of glass, as far as I could tell it was the same one I'd found in the rocks last Sunday morning. I handed it to Phil and he looked at it and then back at Laine and me.

"It's thick, like a lens of some kind or a headlight cover," Laine said. "I suppose it would take an expert to be sure exactly what it's from but it's sure not from a water glass or a vacuum bottle. I suppose it might be from the bottom of a gallon jug, something like that."

"Neither of you saw any footprints or holes by the side of the road where stakes to hold a pair of headlights strung across the road were driven in?" Phil asked.

Laine and I both shook our heads.

"We looked for footprints, naturally, but there'd been some cattle around and all kinds of people," Laine explained. "The ambulance crew, Marge and I, the deputies, my idiot cousin Brad."

I glanced apologetically at Laine, then said, "It almost seemed as if Brad was trying to obscure the tire tracks, the way he squirreled around. It crossed my mind that he might have wanted to account for tire tracks from his car being there."

"I thought of that, too," Laine said. "In fact, he would be my first choice for a murder suspect."

"Mine, too," Audrey added. "I hate to badmouth your relatives, Laine, but that Brad is a real jerk."

"I know," Laine agreed. "He always has been."

"It just about has to be someone close to Mr. Crittenden," Phil said. "Not necessarily a member of the family but someone who lives nearby and who knew him well."

"Well enough to want to kill him," Laine amended. "I know. There aren't many motives for murder and the only one I can think of for murdering Grandpa, is money. That puts it right square in the family. Grandpa was very rich, you know, but he was also very generous. He had given all his children big chunks of money and seen all the grandchildren through college, if they wanted to go, or given them money to start businesses if they didn't, or buy homes." Laine made a gesture of futility. "We all knew if we needed money, we could go to Grandpa. He didn't just fork over for every little thing we wanted but anything we really needed, we knew he'd see we got it."

"Have you seen his will?" I asked. "Maybe it enters into the situation."

"Yes, I've read it. I don't see how it could be a factor, though."

Neither Phil nor I wanted to ask right flat out what was in Paul Crittenden's will but it seemed that we ought to know if we were going to get to the bottom of things.

Laine explained. "He left his money to his kids and grandkids. There's no surprise there. He was a family man. He left an annuity for Ricki Fenton." He told Phil, "She's been his housekeeper for the last six or seven years; since her husband died."

"How did the husband die?" Phil asked. "Accident or illness or what?"

"You really have the most suspicious mind of anyone I ever knew," Laine growled. "I refuse to believe that Ricki is a cold-blooded murderer. Besides, she was at the house all that evening. I know because I was there, too."

"You weren't in the kitchen with her the whole time were you?" I asked. "I mean, she wasn't actually in your sight from the end of supper to when you went out to look for your grandfather?"

"No, of course not. But, damn it, she wouldn't kill

Grandpa. She was fond of him, she fussed over him, tried to make him take it easy, things like that."

"All right," Phil said, taking the bull by the horns, "who does have an alibi and who doesn't?"

Chapter 11

"No one has an alibi worth anything," Laine said. "Everyone was either by themselves or vouched for by someone who would lie for them."

"Can't we eliminate anyone?" Phil asked. "Surely we can eliminate the women. Women don't set booby traps like that, do they? I would think they'd go for poison or a push down the stairs or a butcher knife in the back."

"Hey!" I protested. "This murder is particularly cowardly but women don't hold exclusive rights on cowardice, you know."

"I didn't exactly mean that," Phil said soothingly. "I only meant that most women aren't mechanically minded and this seems to indicate a familiarity with mechanics and explosives."

I accepted that but pointed out that everything used was completely ordinary and it would not be difficult to find out exactly how to use materials readily at hand as they had been used.

Laine nodded. "She's right, Phil. There was nothing that a screwdriver and a crescent wrench wouldn't take care of. Very simple and direct."

Phil stood up. "Come on, it's past lunch time and I'm starved. Let's go see what Mom's got in the fridge."

"I've got sandwich makings," I offered, "and macaroni salad."

"Thanks, Marge," Phil said. "But we ought to go see what Dad found out when he called Kinzua. I expect the sheriff's on his way out now."

"Probably," I agreed. "You guys go on and I'll come down in a little while. I've got a couple of things to do here first."

After the others had gone, I did a little Saturday cleaning and mopped my bedroom floor, as well as the kitchen floor. My mattress was still damp from the water I'd poured on the fire the night before so I couldn't make it up just yet. My laundry would have to wait one more Saturday, there wasn't time to wash and hang it out so it would dry today. Sometimes, in the winter, I have to leave it on the line overnight or even two nights to freeze dry, but whenever possible, I like to bring it in the same day I hang it out.

I made myself a salami sandwich and ate it with some macaroni salad and a glass of tomato juice. Then I shrugged into a cardigan and walked over to

169

Uncle Miles' and Aunt Genevieve's. The five of them were still at the kitchen table, although the lunch dishes had been cleared away and were reposing in the drainer, to be put away when they were dry. I brought the chair from the back porch, where Uncle Miles generally sat to pull his work boots on and off.

"What have I missed?" I asked, glancing around.

They were all looking very solemn and thoughtful. Uncle Miles lit a cigarette and blew a long plume of smoke at the ceiling.

"Not much, honey," Uncle Miles said. "We're trying to account for everyone who might be thought to have a motive."

"Mom's made a list," Phil said. "Why don't you look at it and see if anything strikes you about it?"

"Anyone we've missed or left out," Laine added.

Aunt Genevieve handed me her list of names.

Paul's three children, Elmyra Boggs, Lorena Winton, and Laine's father, Mace. Their spouses and children. Four of the latter were grown up and might be considered to have motives; I was glad to see that Laine was not included in the list of suspects, either from tact or a conviction that matched my own that he was incapable of murdering his grandfather, even if he had wanted to, which I also refused to believe. The two little ones, Laine's half-brother and half-sister, were far too young at six and four. But Mace's two step-daughters were included, although they were only in their teens. Then there were various spouses and girlfriends and boyfriends of the grandchildren. It was a pretty wide field.

"Do any of these people have definite alibis?" I asked. "Besides you, Laine. I know where you were."

Laine shook his head. "No, you don't. Not really. You were riding in the arena, you don't really know where I was while you were riding."

That kind of startled me. I knew he loved his grandfather and I couldn't imagine that he would do anything to harm him.

"No, you're right, Laine," I said, "I don't really know. All the same, I don't believe for one minute that you would do anything to hurt your grandfather or me, either. Uncle Miles, is Mr. Hamilton going to send the police out about my little adventure last night?"

"He said he'd call the sheriff's office in Fossil. He wasn't sure who would claim jurisdiction, the sheriff or the state police, but I think we can expect someone to come out this afternoon."

"The jar and what's left of the rag are in a box on the back porch," Aunt Genevieve said. "I don't see how it will help them -- the rag is just a piece of charred cloth and the jar is just an ordinary quart canning jar, mostly black from the fire."

171

I shuddered involuntarily. Phil put his hand over mine and patted it. I smiled my thanks at him.

"Margie, you're going to sleep here again tonight," Aunt Genevieve ordered.

"But, Aunt -- "

She didn't wait for me to protest. "Not a word. I know you are independent and brave and all the rest of it but you will sleep here tonight."

"Yes, Aunt Genevieve. Thank you."

I glanced at Audrey and she was smiling at me in an understanding sort of way. I thought she must have relatives who fussed over her so she knew how it was a lovely feeling of security and simultaneously an exasperating feeling of being kept a small child forever.

"All right," Aunt Genevieve said. "Now, let's get on with our roster of suspects and alibis. Can we pinpoint where everyone was?"

"Brad and his girlfriend were in the barn," I offered. "I heard Mr. Crittenden exchange a few words with them when he left. But I don't know what time they left, I was concentrating on my riding."

"What about the others? Your two aunts and their husbands?" Uncle Miles asked Laine.

"Elmyra and Leroy were at the house. I tried to get a fix on where they were exactly and what they were doing but I didn't have any luck. Ricki Fenton,

172

our housekeeper, was busy cooking supper, she thought they were in the living room but she didn't know that Brad and Marsha had gone out to the barn so we can't go by that. Lorena and El live in Leavenworth, Kansas but they showed up the next day, with their daughter Janet and her husband. At first I thought they had flown in but Marge pointed out that their car had Kansas tags. They had decided to come out for a visit and surprise us. They said they spent the night in Bend because it was too late when they got there to come out to the ranch." Laine made a gesture of frustration. "So they were close enough to set a booby trap for an old man."

"They couldn't all be in on it," Aunt Genevieve protested. "No murderer takes three accomplices."

"Of course not, Mom," Phil said, looking at Laine, "but one pair of them could have driven to the ranch without the other pair knowing."

"I don't believe it," I said. "I don't believe that any of them drove clear from Kansas with a pair of headlights and a battery ready to kill Paul Crittenden. It's monstrous."

"Sure it is," Uncle Miles agreed, grinding his cigarette out in the ashtray. "It's monstrous no matter who did it. It was monstrous to throw a fire bomb at you, too. I agree that it doesn't seem too likely that folks would come all the way from Kansas with all the paraphernalia to set that booby trap but they wouldn't have to. No doubt there are plenty of headlights and batteries at the ranch and either of the women would know where to lay her hands on them and the necessary tools. How about that, Laine, did you check your equipment for a broken headlight that you couldn't account for?"

Laine nodded. "I checked. There was nothing that I could see. No broken headlights or missing batteries. Nothing that looked as if it had been tampered with."

"Well, at least your dad is out of it," Phil said. "That's one good thing."

Laine gave a wintry little smile. "Yeah, I'm thankful for that. I don't see how the other cousins could be guilty, either. Nadine and Pam and their husbands were home when Aunt Elmyra called to let them know. Nadine lives in Palo Alto and Pam lives in Kansas City."

There was a knock at the front door and Aunt Genevieve went to answer it. She ushered in Mr. Hamilton, the general manager of the corporation, and a Wheeler County deputy sheriff. We all got up and went into the living room. Mr. Hamilton introduced the deputy, Les Wagstaff, and Uncle Miles introduced the rest of us.

Deputy Wagstaff said he wanted to see the scene

174

of the crime before discussing it so he and Mr. Hamilton and Uncle Miles and I walked up to my house.

I showed them the bedroom and the broken window. Mr. Hamilton was horrified and outraged to think such a thing had happened to a school teacher in one of his cottages. It seemed to kind of upset his equilibrium; to his way of thinking the most innocent segment of society in the safest environment possible had been attacked. I agreed with him completely and so did Uncle Miles. Deputy Sheriff Wagstaff, on the other hand, was outraged that I had cleaned everything up.

"You've destroyed all the evidence, Miss O'Connor," he said accusingly. "You've swept up all the glass and stripped the bed. There's nothing to go on."

"I guess I was a little thoughtless," I admitted. "I not only swept the floor but mopped it, as well. But I don't see what it could have told you."

"Physical evidence tells all sorts of things," the deputy said. "Whether the window was broken from the outside or the inside, what was used to break it, the direction it came from, if a rock or other missile was used. All sorts of things."

He shook his head mournfully, looking around the room.

"I hope you don't think I broke the window myself," I said with some acerbity, "and set fire to a treasured heirloom."

"Now, Margie," Uncle Miles said, "take it easy."

I gave him a look. It was easy for him to say, no one suspected him of whatever was on the deputy's mind. What did he think, anyway, that I was some kind of firebug or notoriety fiend? The more I thought about it, the madder I got. I went over to the nightstand and picked up the rock that I'd found on the bed when I had gathered things up to put in the laundry basket. It was just an ordinary stone to me, though I had no doubt whatever that either of the Miller twins could have told us what kind of rock it was, igneous or calciferous or whatever, and identified the geologic epoch it came from, as well. I handed it to Deputy Wagstaff. He looked at me quizzically.

"I found that on the bed this morning," I told him. "Obviously, it was thrown through the window to break it for the bomb."

"It may be obvious to you, miss," the deputy retorted, "but it isn't obvious to me. All I have is a rock and your word, which is really only guesswork, isn't it? It's too bad you didn't leave everything as it was for proper investigation."

"Well, that thing wouldn't take fingerprints

176

anyway," I said, defensively.

"Probably not," he said. "but it's been contaminated as evidence now, whatever we find on it. Just the same, I'd like to preserve it from further contamination. Do you have a clean paper bag I might have?"

I got the deputy a paper grocery bag and he solemnly placed the rock inside and folded the bag around it.

"Do you need to see my bedding?" I asked coldly.

"If you please. You haven't washed it, have you?"

"Not yet. I haven't had time."

I took the blanket and quilt out of the laundry basket and spread them over the mattress, putting the blanket down first to keep the mattress clean. The quilt had been burned clear through in a big, irregular pattern in the center and the blanket was scorched correspondingly. Deputy Wagstaff squinted from the quilt to the window and the window to the quilt, back and forth from different angles until I could have screamed from sheer irritation. He took his forensic camera out of its case and took a number of pictures, ejecting the flashbulbs on the floor. It was so completely obvious what had happened and he was being so nonsensically thorough, I was getting fed up. Uncle Miles finally, after a good look at my face, suggested that we go outside and look at the trajectory from there.

Whoever had thrown the bomb the night before had rolled my chopping block from its place at the front corner of the house over to a position right under my bedroom window and had apparently stood on it to throw the Molotov cocktail. Deputy Wagstaff examined the block from every point, measuring with his eye the distances and angles.

"The window is so high," he said, "that even a tall man would need to stand on something in order to see in and take aim."

"But if he could see in well enough to aim, why didn't he see that Marge wasn't in the bed?" Uncle Miles asked.

The deputy shrugged. "Hard to say." He looked at me. "Was there a light on anywhere in the house?"

"No."

"By the way, why weren't you in bed? It was pretty late for you to be up, wasn't it?"

"I had been in bed," I explained patiently, "but I woke up about one o'clock, a little after one. I don't know what woke me, a sound or just a feeling but I woke up scared. I jumped out of bed and just then the window smashed and the bomb came sailing in and set the bed afire. I had presence of mind enough to grab a pan and fill it with water and douse the flames. Then I heard Mr. Price, Cleve Price, yelling outside. He and his wife are my nearest neighbors. He chased the pyromaniac but lost him among the trees and houses."

"I'll want to talk to him," the deputy said.

"Sure." I pointed out which was the Prices' house. "I expect they're home now, their car is there beside the house."

Deputy Wagstaff spoke to Uncle Miles. "I'll stop by and pick up the rest of the evidence on my way out, sir."

Uncle Miles nodded. "It'll be there for you."

The deputy put his notebook in his pocket and thanked us for our cooperation then went over to Prices', carrying the rock in the paper bag.

"Margie," Uncle Miles said, "let's take that wet bedding and throw it over the clothesline to dry."

I nodded, wondering what I could have been thinking to just leave it in the laundry basket. I rolled the quilt and blanket together and he carried them for me. Together we put them on the line, throwing them over two lines in order to leave space between the folds so they would dry faster. Then we went inside.

"Marge," Phil said as I came into the kitchen, "Laine and Audrey are going back home now but I want to see the lay of the land where the accident happened. You want to go with me tomorrow?"

179

"Sure. Maybe it'll give you some ideas that'll help."

"That's what I'm hoping," Laine said.

He stood up and so did Phil. Uncle Miles shook hands with him and said he was glad to have met him. Aunt Genevieve smiled at him and patted his arm, inviting him to come back anytime, including Audrey in the invitation and the smile. Phil and I walked out to the pickup with them.

"We'll be out at your place around one or so," Phil said to Laine. "That okay with you, Marge?"

"Fine. We'll need to get back here fairly early, I've got school Monday morning, you know," I reminded them.

"One is just about right for me, too. Aunt Elmyra and Aunt Lorena are still at the house. The rest of the folks have gone home but they're hell-bent on dividing up what they call the 'family heirlooms' and they're both scared to death that one of 'em's going to get more than the other. I'm seriously thinking of moving over to the Riverside Motel until they're gone. And Ricki's on the verge of quitting. I finally told her to take a couple of weeks off until the old girls get tired of fighting and go home."

We all laughed and Laine joined in rather ruefully. I shook my head sadly. I always feel it's such a shame for a family to get bogged down in that kind of morass on the death of a parent. Those can be the meanest battles and leave the most scars on a family of any fighting. I was so grateful that my brother and sister and I had been able to avoid the most acrimonious conflicts when we'd settled our parents' estate. Not that we didn't have a certain amount of tugging and pulling, but we didn't do any lasting damage to our relationships.

Laine and Audrey got in the pickup and Laine rolled his window down. "I'll see you tomorrow, then," he said, and started the engine.

"Okay," Phil said. "Take it easy on the way home."

They both waved as Laine pulled onto the road and started up the hill; Phil and I waved back. Then we went into the house. Uncle Miles was in his recliner reading *Members of the Family* by Owen Wister. He'd read it several times before but he never seemed to get tired of it. Aunt Genevieve was sitting in her special chair, crocheting something white and ruffled. I assumed at first it was a doily but as I sat on the end of the couch and looked more closely, it didn't look like one. Phil went into the kitchen and came back with an opened beer bottle.

"Anyone else for a beer or anything?" he asked politely.

"No, thanks," Aunt Genevieve said.

"Yes, by golly, I'll have one," Uncle Miles said, glancing up from his book.

"Not for me," I answered.

Phil brought a beer and handed it to Uncle Miles, then sat down on the other end of the couch.

"What's that you're crocheting?" I asked. "It's not a doily, is it?"

Aunt Genevieve smiled. "Nope. It's an Easter dress for Lacey."

She held it up and I could see that it was a tiny skirt. Lacy is her granddaughter and is about eighteen months old. She's a real go-getter and I figured she'd probably ruin the dress the first time she wore it but that was Aunt Genevieve's lookout.

"It's lovely," I said, keeping my misgivings to myself.

"There's a pink pique dress and this skirt goes over it. There's a crocheted collar, too, if I have time to get it done."

"She'll be the best-dressed tyke in church," I said.

There was a knock on the door and Phil went to open it. Deputy Wagstaff took off his hat and stepped inside. He was empty-handed so he must have put his camera and the rock in his patrol car.

He nodded at Aunt Genevieve and me, dividing a "ma'am" between us. Uncle Miles put his book down and stood up.

"The jar and rag are out on the back porch. Go get them, will you, Phil?"

"Don't do that," The deputy exclaimed, grimacing. "They've been handled too much already. I'll just go get them myself."

"All right," Uncle Miles said agreeably. "Phil, show the deputy to the back porch?"

Phil grinned and led the way, opening the porch door and gesturing at the jar where it sat in a small box in the dry laundry tub. The charred rag wick was inside the jar. Deputy Wagstaff came back through the living room carefully carrying the box with its seemingly precious evidence. I didn't see what good it was going to do anyone. Every house in camp -- shoot, probably every house in Oregon -- had canning jars, even the bunkhouses. They were used for everything from canning fruit to storing nails to displaying marble and seashell collections.

I couldn't see how even the crime lab expected to distinguish one jar from all the rest to tell where it had come from and who had used it as a bomb. The fire had destroyed any possibility of fingerprints or stray hairs or tell-tale unique kinds of dust. The little piece of charred rag was about as useful, as far as I could tell. Even if the lab identified the cloth, there wouldn't be anything to say who it had belonged to. We already knew it was in Camp Five so it was available to anyone who cared to take the trouble to snitch it no matter who had originally owned it. But it made Deputy Wagstaff happy to take it and it didn't hurt anything.

He had a few questions that he'd thought of after his talk with Cleve Price. I answered them as best I could but I didn't really think they were going to be any more useful than the physical evidence he'd collected. He finally left and I watched him through the window as he delicately placed the box in his patrol car trunk and then got in under the wheel and drove away.

"Come on, Phil," I said. "Let's go over to my place. I want to pack a bag for tonight."

After dinner had been eaten and the dishes taken care of, Phil suggested a drive. Uncle Miles and Aunt Genevieve passed so just the two of us went. I took my purse along in case of certain feminine emergencies and Phil took his revolver in case of certain masculine ones.

The nearest church was in Fossil, about thirty miles away, but I don't know anything that induces a more worshipful, reverent attitude than deep woods at twilight. Phil took a right turn onto the main road but soon turned off onto an old dirt road. The light was beginning to fail but it was not yet dark enough to need headlights. It wasn't long before we came to a ford on Thirtymile Creek. This was a place we both knew well and loved. Phil stopped the pickup short of the ford and turned off the motor. We both got out and walked upstream, deeper into the woods.

There was a log on the bank just below a small rapids. We sat down and watched the creek thrash its way noisily down through the boulders, white water on top, green water beneath. Up above the rapids a doe and her twin fawns stepped daintily out of the trees to the creek. They looked and sniffed the air but we were sitting very still and they didn't see us. They drank deeply and walked upstream and back into the woods. When it was almost totally dark, Phil and I started back to the pickup. We hadn't said a word since we left Camp Five and we didn't speak until we were back on the front porch.

"Thanks," I whispered. "That was sublime."

"You're welcome," my cousin whispered as he opened the door.

Chapter 12

It was heavenly to curl up in my cousin Lorraine's bed that Saturday night. I had slept in it many times before, when we were children and I'd spent weekends and even weeks during the summer visiting Uncle Miles and Aunt Genevieve, but never had I been conscious of feeling so safe and protected. Uncle Miles had been a Seabee in the Pacific Theater in World War II and my cousin Phil was a rodeo cowboy, the two of them ought to be enough protection for any woman. But I didn't like feeling like a refugee; I didn't like the knowledge that it was fear that kept me from my own home. On the other hand, I liked even less serving as a target for Molotov cocktails.

Although I was tired with all the strain and excitement and lack of sleep of the last twenty-four hours, I didn't fall asleep at once. I would doze a bit, then come back to full consciousness, and look around the room and at the windows, which, like my own bedroom windows were very small and high. A couple of times I heard cars going past and once it seemed that one stopped nearby and went silent, as if it had been parked. I wondered vaguely when no sound of a car door shutting followed. The room was dark, a big old lilac bush at the corner of the house shaded the windows so they were only pale gray. I thought about getting a dog. It would be a relief to know that I would have some warning of visitors or intruders but I planned to do a little traveling in the summer and it would be difficult to take a dog with me. Thinking of the best breed of dog for my purposes, I fell into a doze.

Suddenly, I woke with a start. The parade of dogs -- collies, weimeraners, fox terriers, cocker spaniels, basset hounds -- was scattered as I struggled to focus on whatever had awakened me. I had been more deeply asleep than I thought and the dogs confused me, especially as I could hear one barking. At first I thought it was part of the dream, then I realized it was nearby, outside. After a couple of moments, I identified Duchess, the Worleys' cocker spaniel. I blinked rapidly, trying to see through the darkness. The windows were still gray rectangles. I had a feeling of urgency that I couldn't account for. It was a feeling of something left undone that was important for me to do. Oh, of course! My purse. I'd left it in

Phil's pickup. It would be perfectly safe there until morning but it had my grandmother's diamond ring in it. It was of no very great monetary value but it figured largely in the family chronicles and I would hate to lose it. I didn't ordinarily carry it around in my purse but I hadn't wanted to leave it at home with the house under attack. I knew I wouldn't get back to sleep until I retrieved it and had it safely in the room with me.

I looked at the clock and saw that it wasn't all that late, only a few minutes past eleven. I swung my legs around and sat up. I didn't want to go outside in the dark alone. I thought about waking Phil up to ask him to go with me. That idea died a-borning. I knew he would do it but there was not a chance that I would give Phil such an opportunity to tease me. Besides, I had my pride. I would not be such a coward that I couldn't go to a pickup parked practically right outside the door. I put my robe and slippers on and padded out to the front door. I knew the house well and didn't need to light the way to the front door.

I closed the door softly behind me. The scattered clouds allowed just enough moonlight to see the shape of Phil's pickup outside the fence. I don't know when Duchess stopped barking but I remember the silence of the night as I went down the walk. Just as I put my hand on the door handle, I heard a soft sound behind me and to my left. I whirled around and all hell broke loose. There was a swishing sound and I saw a dark person-sized mass loom up beside me. I had time for one yell before I felt a cord being passed around my neck. I clawed at the arms holding the cord and, gasping and choking, I kept trying to scream. The hands relaxed their hold and I tried to break away but something hit me on the side of the head. It didn't knock me out but it confused me still further. Adding to my befuddlement, my Grandma Straversky came momentarily to mind. I fell to my knees and as I fought to get away, more blows fell on my shoulders and back.

Uncle Miles called out but I couldn't understand what he said. All I could understand was that if I didn't get help, I was going to be killed right then and there. I could hear my assailant's breath, ragged and heavy. As suddenly as the attack had started, it ended and I was alone on the ground beside Phil's pickup. The porch light came on and I heard Uncle Miles and Phil coming down the walk. I dragged myself to a sitting position and put my hand to the back of my head.

Phil, wearing only a pair of briefs, got to me first by a short head. Aunt Genevieve, in her nightgown, came right behind Uncle Miles, who was wearing

189

pajama bottoms but no top. There were a lot of horrified exclamations and questions, none of which I could answer. My head was bleeding and my shoulders and back hurt.

"Stay with Marge, Dad," Phil said.

He ran back to the house and I heard the sound of a motor starting up nearby. The sound seemed to excite Uncle Miles and I was about to ask him why when I realized it must be my assailant making a getaway. That made me mad.

"Go help Phil, I'm all right," I said.

At least that's what I intended to say, but from the look on Uncle Miles' face, I didn't enunciate it very clearly. He and Aunt Genevieve helped me to my feet and inside. They sat me down at the kitchen table and Aunt Genevieve brought towels, covered my shoulders with one and made a pad for my head with the other. She put my hand up to hold it in place and told me to keep it there. I caught a glimpse of Phil, fully dressed and buckling on his holster with the pearl-handled revolver he'd bought to complete his cowboy image. He ran out the front door and I heard the it slam and his pickup start up and race up the hill to the main road.

The rest of that night is pretty hazy in my memory. My head hurt something fierce and Aunt Genevieve wouldn't give me anything for it because she was afraid of concussion or even fracture and wanted to keep me awake. She clipped the hair around the cut and bandaged my head. She said it should have a couple of stitches but I refused to go to the hospital. The nearest one was in Heppner, forty miles away, and my hair would hide the scar. Aunt Genevieve moved me into the bathroom and washed the cuts on my back and shoulders and dressed them. Then she got me into a clean pair of pajamas and a clean robe. After I changed I went out to the living room and Uncle Miles put me in his recliner. He had donned a bathrobe at some point while Aunt Genevieve was busy with me. He sat down and lit a cigarette, squinting at me through the smoke.

"Well, Margie, another exciting night."

"I'm sorry, Uncle Miles."

"Don't be silly. You have nothing to be sorry for. But someone has and I'd hate to be him when Phil catches up to him."

Aunt Genevieve came in, wearing her robe and with her hair neatly combed.

"Margie, I think you'd better stay out here for a little while, until we see just what we're dealing with. Can you see all right? Is there any blurry vision or double vision?"

"No, I'm fine. You and Uncle Miles go back to bed."

191

"Don't be silly," Aunt Genevieve said, repeating Uncle Miles. "I'm going to make some tea and some cocoa for Margie. Miles, would you like something?"

"Tea is fine," he said.

I was still so shaky that when Aunt Genevieve brought my cocoa, she had to take it back and bring me only half a cupful so I wouldn't slop it all over the place. I was describing what had happened, or what I thought had happened, for the fourth or fifth time when Phil's pickup pulled up in front of the house and he came in. He looked very grim and angry. We all looked at him with the one paramount question in our faces.

"No, I didn't catch the son of a bitch." He glanced at his mother. "Sorry, Mom. No, I didn't catch the malefactor. But I did find where he's been hiding."

He flung himself down on the couch and Aunt Genevieve looked at him speculatively.

"Would you like a cup of tea or cocoa, Son?" she asked.

He stood up and grinned at her.

"No, thanks. I'd like something with a little bite to it. How about you, Dad?"

Uncle Miles shook his head. "Tea'll do me."

Phil went into the kitchen and came back with a highball.

"Well?" I demanded. "Where has this wretch

been hiding?"

"Camp Six," Phil said. "Ideal for the purpose. Close enough to Camp Five to run over whenever a spot of mayhem seems indicated, far enough from Camp Five -- and, incidentally from any other human habitation -- for privacy and secrecy. There aren't many buildings left but a couple of them are still sound enough to use if you're not too fastidious. Since it's on the old railroad line, it's far enough off the main road that lights wouldn't give him away. All he had to do was watch for traffic on the main road and his comings and goings would be invisible to all intents and purposes."

We all understood what Phil meant. There had been a number of logging camps scattered along the railway line years ago when the corporation brought the logs into the sawmill by rail. Camp Five is the only one left intact and it's still here only because of its location on the main hauling road. The others have been gone for years, all except a few houses at Camp Six.

"How did you manage to find that out?" Aunt Genevieve asked. "Did you follow him clear in?"

"No, he had too much of a head start. I took a wild guess at the top of the hill, at the junction of our road and the main road. There are only two ways he could go so I had a fifty-fifty chance. I took the right and pretty near floorboarded the old pickup, hoping to catch a glimpse of his headlights ahead of me. I didn't but on the way back, I got to thinking about where he's been these past couple of days. No one in camp has seen any strangers hanging around but I figured he must have stayed close, to prowl around and find out where Margie lived and to find out something about her routine.

"If he'd been staying in Fossil, people would have noticed him coming out here. So I thought of Camp Six and when I came to the turnoff for it, I went in." He laughed. "I must have looked pretty funny -- I left the pickup in a thicket of young firs and walked the last half mile. There wasn't anyone there but I turned my flashlight on and looked in the cabins. One of them had been swept and there were fresh ashes in the trashburner. The stovepipe wasn't all there but he had poked a section of it out the window. There were also some fresh cans and bottles in a wooden box in back. Maybe that deputy can come tomorrow and collect some fingerprints."

Phil yawned and finished his drink. I was calmer but still very angry.

"Well, I just don't get it," I objected. "Why me? Why the hell would anyone want to murder me?"

"Calm down, Margie," Aunt Genevieve cautioned. "Excitement isn't good for head injuries."

"I wish you'd make whoever attacked me understand that," I said.

Phil laughed and Uncle Miles grinned at me. But he was sober enough a moment later.

"Honey, why would anyone want to hurt you?" Uncle Miles asked seriously.

"I don't know. Unless whoever killed Paul Crittenden thinks I know something detrimental to him -- something incriminating."

"Do you?" Phil asked.

"No. No, I don't. Not one single solitary thing," I wailed.

"As I understand it," Phil said, "you heard someone in some nearby rocks that night. Did you say or do anything to make him think you knew who it was?"

I shook my head and regretted it immediately. The face I made caused Aunt Genevieve to come over and take my pulse.

"No, I don't think so. I don't see how I could have since I didn't see anyone and wasn't even sure of what I heard. It could have been a coyote or a bobcat or even a cow, for that matter. I did call out but I only asked who was there."

"Still, the person might have thought you could see much better than you really could," Uncle Miles suggested.

195

"I suppose," I agreed, grudgingly.

"How much did you see of this guy tonight?" Phil asked.

"Not much. Just a sort of shape, you know. A dark mass is all. The moon was pretty much covered by clouds just then so I really only saw the person as a sort of amorphous movement."

"How big, Margie?" Aunt Genevieve, apparently satisfied with my heart rate, went to sit in her easy chair. "Describe it, not only what you saw but what you felt, what you smelled, what you heard."

"You didn't happen to bite him, did you?" Phil asked with a grin. "If you did, you can tell us how he tasted."

I shot my cousin a sour look. Then I gave Aunt Genevieve's suggestions some serious thought. Some rather surprising ideas came to mind. Smell -- some kind of talcum. I couldn't quite isolate the smell but it made me think of talcum powder. As for what I felt, I had the bandages to show for that, there wasn't much mystery there. What I heard hadn't amounted to much, there hadn't been any speech, just grunts and gasps and heavy breathing. Yes, but that made me think of someone I'd met just recently. Laine's mother breathed hard just normally, without any particularly strenuous activity.

"I didn't see much of the person, you know," I

said slowly. "I just got a kind of impression of a bulky shadow."

"Tall, short, fat, thin?" Uncle Miles asked.

"Not tall," I said, trying to see again with my mind's eye. "Not thin. I think shorter than me." That surprised me and I ran the scene in my head again as best I could. "Yes, shorter than me. But broad."

"Right, that's what you're describing, Marge," Phil said. "A broad."

Aunt Genevieve protested. "Phil, please. Not a broad, a woman."

"Sorry, Mom. But if this person was shorter than Marge, well, not many men are that short. She's not a tall girl."

"And talcum powder," added Uncle Miles. "That sounds like a woman."

"Well, men do use talcum powder," said Aunt Genevieve.

"Satin Rose," I exclaimed, triumphantly. "That's what this person smelled like. Grandma Straversky always used it, that's why she came to mind while I was fighting with whoever it was."

"What is it, Margie?" Uncle Miles asked softly.

My face evidently showed that I had remembered where I had recently encountered Satin Rose talcum powder. When Laine and I had gone to visit his mother, I had used her lavatory and there was a can

197

of it on the shelf beside the sink.

"I know who it was," I said, with no triumph whatever.

My aunt and uncle and cousin looked at me expectantly.

"It was Laine's mother," I said sadly.

I had to explain to them how I had arrived at that conclusion. In my own mind I was quite sure that she was my assailant. She was short and heavyset and kind of pathetic. Somehow my anger was gone and I felt only heavy sadness and deep sorrow. This was going to hit a good man hard.

"No, I can't prove any of it," I agreed with Uncle Miles, "but I know it's true."

"What about a motive?" asked Phil.

"Money. Always and forever, money. She's never had much but Paul Crittenden loaned her the money to buy a motel out of Bend, on the Deschutes. She didn't like running it, she said so that day I was there with Laine. I'm sure she thought either that Paul had left her some money in his will or she was confident that she could get it from Laine, once Paul was dead. As I'm sure she could."

Aunt Genevieve nodded. "A combination of greed, pride, and self-pity. That could work out to murder in certain circumstances."

She came over to me and shone a pencil

198

flashlight in my eyes and took my pulse again. She was evidently satisfied with what she found.

"Okay, Margie," she said. "Let's get you to bed. Let's all go to bed. Things will look better in the morning."

I was just reaching out to turn off the lamp beside the bed, a china lady in a yellow crinoline skirt with a ruffled shade, when there was a knock on the door.

"Come in."

Phil came in and handed me my purse.

"So you won't have any excuse to go out and get yourself beaned again," he said.

"I suppose you think I like getting beaned and beaten up," I said.

I opened my purse and took out the little worn velvet-lined jeweler's box and opened it. Grandma's ring winked up at us with tiny points of petrified fire.

"A thing as beautiful as that is worth getting beat up for," Phil remarked.

"Speaking of getting beaten up, what did she hit me with? Do you know?"

Phil looked at me guiltily. "Promise you won't tell Mom?"

Puzzled but curious, I promised.

"First, I think she hit you with the side of my pickup. I mean, she threw you against it when you fought her. At least that's how the side of your head

199

and face look."

I lightly touched the side of my face and winced.

"Okay," I said. "That seems right. First she tried to strangle me with some kind of cord and when I fought back she dropped the cord and shoved me hard. I was off-balance and fell sideways against your pickup then to the ground. After that she started to hit me with a club or something."

"It was a broken pitchfork handle. I ran over mine a couple of months ago and just tossed the tines in the back of the pickup and stuck the handle in the hole in the wall of the bed, back of the cab on the driver's side. When she needed a weapon, there it was. Unfortunately, it was the kind that has a metal grip on the end -- that's what did most of the damage to you. I'm sorry, Marge."

I laughed. It was a shaky kind of laugh and ended with something that was perilously close to a sob.

"Come on, Phil, it isn't your fault. If that handle hadn't been handy she might have found something even worse. What I can't understand is why she didn't conk me first and then strangle me."

"Is she a very intelligent bro...woman?"

"No, I don't think so. Normal I.Q., I think."

"Well, she probably goes to a lot of movies. Strangling looks easy in the movies, you know. Run a cord across someone's throat, pull it tight, and the

200

person keels over. No muss, no fuss, quick and painless. She was probably very surprised that you didn't react correctly."

"Yes, well, I'll try to remember the script better next time."

Phil leaned down and kissed my cheek, hugging me close for a moment.

"There'd better not be a next time," he said. "You go to sleep now."

"I will. You, too. Goodnight."

Chapter 13

In spite of the excitements of the night before, I woke at my usual time on Sunday morning. My upper body was stiff and painful when I moved and it ached when I didn't move. I had a pretty intense headache, too. I went into the bathroom and took three aspirin tablets, avoiding looking in the mirror and wishing I had something stronger. I would ask Aunt Genevieve for something when she was up and around. I went back to my room and very slowly and carefully, put on a pair of slacks and a sweater.

Uncle Miles and Aunt Genevieve slept late on Sundays, as they had to get up at 4:30 on weekday mornings. It was eight o'clock by the time Aunt Genevieve had breakfast underway and the delicious aromas of perking coffee and frying ham pulled me to the kitchen. I set the table and got milk and plum conserves and raspberry jelly from the refrigerator. Aunt Genevieve's conserve recipe called for thinly sliced lemons and chopped walnuts and was food fit for the gods but as stiff and sore as my jaw was when I bade her good morning, I knew I would be limiting my chewing for a couple of days. I would make out all right with her homemade raspberry jelly on my biscuits.

We all talked the situation over while we ate and Phil decided to go and talk to Laine. Although I was positive in my own mind that his mother was the one who had attacked me last night, I had to agree that my identification was not really proof. Maybe she would have a cast iron alibi. I wanted to go with him and it took quite a lot of insistence on my part to convince the others. At that, I guess they were more worn down by what Phil called my hard-headed stubborn streak than anything else. Aunt Genevieve had given me a few pain pills, two taken at breakfast and the others to be taken at four-hour intervals, as needed, so I felt able to cope with life. I wanted to help with the dishes but Aunt Genevieve shooed me out of the kitchen so Phil and I could get started. As she pointed out, the sooner we got started, the sooner we'd get back. And there was school tomorrow, of course. Sylvia and I had to finish getting everyone ready for the spring program. Four of the boys in my room had decided to form a barbershop quartette and were going to sing a couple of songs. They had settled on "The Fountain in the Park" and "Where

Did You Get that Hat?" after much discussion and had been assiduously rehearsing. I was to accompany them and I had not been assiduously rehearsing. If I didn't want to embarrass myself, I'd have to get in some practice soon.

Then there was Doreen Cranston's recitation. She wanted to recite "Trees," and I hadn't been able to talk her into anything else. "Trees" is such a lovely little poem and I knew that Doreen would make it sound comical, not on purpose but just because she recited in a sing-song voice with the accents, when there were any, in the wrong places. Oh, well, it was at least short so we wouldn't have to suffer long.

Debbie and Dottie Miller had worked out some kind of dialogue. I hadn't heard it yet and while they could be depended upon to be either interesting or entertaining or both, it would behoove me to find out the general outline before unleashing them on the audience. They were very original and I didn't want anything startling from them. At least it would be in English and not Quoskeen; I had made that rule right at the beginning of planning the program.

"You're very quiet this morning," Phil remarked about the time we turned off the logging road onto the highway. "Hurts, doesn't it?"

"As a matter of fact, it is rather painful. I suppose this is how you feel after every ride," I said sympathetically.

To my surprise, he bulled up at that.

"Not every ride," he said testily. "I do manage to stay on the full eight seconds every once in a while."

"Sorry. I didn't mean to imply that you got bucked off every time. I just meant that there's a certain amount of bone shaking with pretty much every ride."

Mollified, he grinned at me. "That's a fact."

"How are we going to handle this thing? I can't very well waltz up to Laine and tell him I'm sure his mother is a murderer."

"I wonder if he suspects her. I don't suppose he'd let on to us, if he did."

"I doubt it. He's pretty close to her. If he does suspect her, he is probably fighting very hard not to."

"Well, I don't know how to broach the subject to him." Phil made a kind of helpless gesture. "I guess we'll just have to play it by ear."

I agreed. We discussed it the rest of the way to the Happy Appy Ranch but didn't get any closer to figuring out how to approach Laine with our suspicions. When we pulled into the driveway and parked in the area between the house and the barn, Laine's pickup was there and so were four cars. I recognized Lorena's Studebaker with its Kansas license plate and Elmyra's pink Olds but the others meant nothing to me. An animated discussion was in progress in the back yard. Laine and five women stood staring at each other. I recognized his two aunts and presumed the two young women were cousins. The woman with her back to us appeared to be about the same vintage as the aunts and I presumed she was Laine's mom.

Laine looked harassed and angry. In fact, as I looked at them more closely, they all looked angry. The older women all seemed to be talking at once, with the younger ones chiming in now and then. No one paid any attention to us at first, they were too busy quarrelling. It was an awkward time for comparative strangers to butt in and Phil muttered that maybe we ought to go and come back later. I was about to voice my agreement when the woman I had guessed to be Laine's mother turned and my guess was confirmed, the lady was indeed Georgia Smith Crittenden.

As she turned, she shouted that she'd see them all in hell first. Then she flounced out the gate, digging in her purse for her car keys. Laine bounded after her, evidently trying to placate her, from the look on his face and his gestures. She withdrew her hand from her purse, the car keys in her grasp and stalked rapidly to her car, an old and shabby Ford sedan. She didn't notice Phil and me until she was almost to the car. I could see the exact split second that she recognized me and took in the bandage around my head -- her face reflected a truly awful concatenation of emotions, of which rage appeared to be the dominant ingredient.

Mrs. Crittenden yanked her car door open and flung herself behind the wheel. In a matter of seconds she had started the car and stamped on the accelerator so hard that she churned up a tall rooster tail of gravel and dirt. The aunts and cousins stood in the yard with their mouths open but Laine ran to us and I barely had time to scramble over to the center of the seat before he was inside yelling for Phil to catch his mom.

Phil needed no further urging. He started the pickup and nearly broke my knee jamming the gear shift into first. I pulled my knee over, out of harm's way, and held onto the seat as best I could as Phil spun a tight circle and raced down the driveway after Mrs. Crittenden.

"What's going on?" Phil asked, leaning forward to look around me at Laine and shoving the gear shift into second.

"My mother and my aunts and cousins have been going round and round all morning," Laine said. "It was bad enough when it was just Aunt Elmyra and Aunt Lorena. The uncles went home right after the funeral, and so did Brad and Marsha. But these women! I've never seen or heard anything like it. I thought the house was full of old junk but it seems everything in it is a priceless antique and all of them want each and every piece. Then my mother got in the act and she says everything belongs to me now because it's all part of the ranch and I'm the surviving partner. I don't give a damn about the stuff, let them take whatever they want. But Mother's upset and I'm afraid she'll wreck, the way she's driving."

"Where's she going?" I asked. "Do you know?"

Laine shook his head. "Not really. I suppose she's going home but I'm not sure. I don't know why she lit out of there like a scalded cat. What the devil happened to you?" he added, nodding at my bandaged cranium and bruised cheek.

I didn't see how I could tell Laine just then. I think Mrs. Crittenden was already upset and just barely under control when the sight of me threw her completely off balance. In spite of my aching body, which Phil's speed and the tightness of his shocks wasn't doing a thing to ameliorate, I felt sorry for her. I felt even sorrier for Laine. Eventually, I would have to tell him about last night and where my suspicions led, just short of absolute certainty. It was going to be an awful blow to him.

Phil had caught up with Mrs. Crittenden by the

time she turned onto the blacktop road. We made the turn just seconds after she did. The speedometer needle was way over on the right as we raced after her and she slowed only enough to make the turn onto Highway 97. The pickup required a bit slower speed to negotiate the turn so there was a car between us when Phil had gotten straightened out.

"She's headed north," Laine exclaimed. "I don't know where she thinks she's going; her place is west of town."

Phil passed the car between us, a family out for a Sunday drive. Mrs. Crittenden had been compelled to slow a bit on 97 because there was a fair amount of traffic. Still, she managed to keep a terrifying pace; I wished for nothing more than for a state trooper to materialize behind her and pull her over. I was completely puzzled as to her intentions and I could see that Phil and Laine were just as much in the dark as I was.

She passed recklessly, scooting back and forth over the center line like a skier on a slalom course, missing head-on collisions by the skin of her teeth again and again. She lengthened her lead, Phil being unwilling to take the risks she was taking, but we caught glimpses of her through the traffic and were only a half mile or so back when she pulled into the wayside area at the south end of the Crooked River

Gorge. She was going too fast as she left the highway and she skidded sideways across the gravel of the parking area. She slammed on the brakes but couldn't stop in time -- the Ford crashed into a rough lava spire, caving in the whole right side of the car and popping the trunk open.

Laine jumped out even before Phil had brought the pickup to a complete stop, and ran toward his mother. She wrenched the driver's side door open and stood for a fleeting moment, looking at Laine with what I can only describe as agonized love. Phil and I got out and stood watching helplessly.

Mrs. Crittenden moved forward swiftly toward the gorge but Laine caught her by the sleeve. I heard the fabric rip as she tore herself free.

"I'm sorry," she screamed at Laine. "I'm sorry."

He lunged for her but a couple of running steps took her to the edge of the precipice and over, eight hundred feet to the bottom. I expect Laine will continue to hear her scream for the rest of his life. I guess Phil and I will, too.

I did my best to comfort Laine but there wasn't really anything I could say or do to mitigate the horror of his loss. After his "no, no, no, no" turned to "why," Phil and I told him about last night.

"I think she must have thought I could identify her from the night your grandfather died," I explained. "And she must have been pretty sure that I could identify her from last night."

Laine nodded.

He led the way over to the Ford and we looked in the trunk. There in coils of haywire were a couple of wooden stakes, a battery, and two headlights, one with a broken lens.

"They're from the old John Deere that we keep in a shed on the upper hayfields," Laine said. We don't use it much, mostly just to pull the hay wagon in the winter when we feed the stock up there. On the way home yesterday I got to thinking about it and that I'd checked all the equipment but that old Johnnypopper. I went up there last night and sure enough, the headlights had been taken off and the battery was gone."

Laine looked at me and then at Phil with the ghost of a rueful smile.

"I thought it was Brad," he said. "I thought it was Brad."

All at once, he lost his composure.

"Why?" he cried. "Why did she have to kill Grandpa? He was ninety-four years old! Why murder a man ninety-four years old?"

Neither Phil nor I had anything to say to that. I had my theory and I'm sure Laine and Phil had theirs. But I don't know of any words that could conceivably be said to tell a man that his mother was a murderer because she was tired of drudgery, of dreary monotony, of loneliness. She knew that if Paul hadn't left her anything in his will, she would be able to get what she wanted from Laine. She knew that Laine had the ranch partnership and she could be very sure that Paul would have left him a sizable chunk of cash, as well.

I put my hand on Laine's arm.

"Laine," I said softly, "Try to think of all this as an illness. Your mother must have lost her mental balance someway. Try to just remember that she loved you so much that in the end she preferred to take a quick way out rather than put you through the agony of seeing her tried for murder."

"Oh, God," he said and began to weep.

About the Author

Barbara J. Olexer is a fourth-generation Oregonian. She has written more than twenty books and screenplays. Her first published book was *The Enslavement of the American Indian*, a nonfiction account of that little-known segment of American history.

Her formative years were spent in small farming towns and a backwoods logging camp. Barbara's life has been a tapestry of changes as she has lived and worked in small Oregon towns, such as Ashland, Camp Five (a logging camp that belonged to Kinzua Pine Mills), Klamath Falls, and Malin, as well as some of the country's biggest cities, such as San Francisco, Hollywood, Baltimore, and Washington, D.C.

On retirement, Barbara joyfully returned to the Pacific Northwest where her two grown sons and her grandchildren live. She lives in Milwaukie, Oregon, with her husband and two cats.

www.ingramcontent.com/pod-product-compliance
Lightning Source LLC
Chambersburg PA
CBHW051649260626
47170CB00004B/1412